Best

I've Ever Had

NEW YORK TIMES BESTSELLING AUTHOR

ABBI GLINES

Best I've Ever Had
Published by Abbi Glines
Copyright © 2019 by Abbi Glines

abbi@abbiglinesbooks.com

Editor:
My Brother's Editor

Interior Design & Formatting by:
Christine Borgford

Best
I've Ever Had

Dedication

Second chances aren't just found in the pages of a book but if you're lucky you'll get one in the real world too.

Thank you, *Britt*, for not letting me walk away, for fighting for me, and most of all for loving me enough.

Best I've Ever Had

Summer had returned. The nightlife lit up the coastal town of Sea Breeze, Alabama with scantily clad sun-kissed bodies, live music, the smell of fresh cooked seafood.

Taking it all in, he wondered if coming back had been the best thing. He wasn't the same man who had driven out of town a year ago on the motorcycle he'd bought after his best friend's wedding. From the messy blonde curls he'd let grow out, to the tattoos now covering his arms, part of his chest and even the side of his neck, it all represented a part of his journey.

Eli Hardy was back, but he didn't plan on staying for long.

Best Friend's Wedding Day

THE WATCH ON my wrist said it was 2:15PM.

The flask tucked in my pocket wasn't half empty because I was broken-hearted about my best friend getting married. I'd come to terms with Bliss marrying Nate Finlay. Hell, I'd fallen in love or I had thought I had with someone else. I still couldn't be sure on that one. It had ended before it even started. The months had gone by and I was over losing her too.

I had decided I was the perpetual good guy. The guy girls know as steady, dependable, forgiving, blah *motherfuckingblah*. I took another swig from my flask at that thought. The rim was cool on my lips surprising me. It wasn't summer yet, but in South Alabama, it might as well be. If they'd chosen to have this thing on the beach, we'd at least have had a good breeze.

Since we were kids, Bliss always said she'd get married here, on her parents' farm just like they had years ago. She thought it was romantic and shit. I thought it was too damn hot and out of the way but I was also drinking and a bit callous on love, at the moment.

"You want to share that?" I recognized that sultry female voice. Once you heard Ophelia Finlay speak, you never forgot how she sounded. The first time I'd met her she'd been the new roommate of the girl I was almost but not quite dating, Lila Carter. Sure, Lila had been the instrument that got me over loving my best friend. But she'd moved right on over me in a blink to a Rosemary Beach rich ass bad boy too.

I handed the flask to Ophelia. I had noticed her earlier, but everyone noticed her. She was hard to miss. Pale blonde hair, blue eyes that I swear looked like they had silver in them, and exceptionally nice tits. I was a drunk man and in that strapless dress, it was hard to ignore. I doubted many females could hold a dress up with their rack the way Ophelia was doing. Ophelia and I didn't really know each other well but she would be my best friend's sister-in-law before the sun set.

I handed her the flask.

"It's whiskey," I told her as she took the flask from me.

I let myself appreciate the view up close. And damn what a view it was.

She cut her eyes at me sharply and underneath her heavy lashes, I saw the gleam of amusement there. "I can handle it."

I'd heard a few stories about her from Bliss. She wasn't the wildest of Nate Finlay's two younger sisters. That title went to Phoenix Finlay. Her red hair was the only warning one got that she was trouble. She looked like an angel. The first time I met her I wondered if they'd made up the stories about her. Then at a birthday party for Bliss that Nate had held at his house, Phoenix had stripped off her clothing all except for a pair of tiny panties and jumped into the pool. Nate had cursed a fucking blue streak while the rest of the males in attendance watched.

"Single malt, mmmm. Thanks, I needed that," Ophelia's voice was so damn warm and raspy. I'd forgotten how much I liked hearing her talk.

"Wedding joy stressing you out?" I asked, taking one more drink before closing it back up and tucking it into my suit coat jacket.

She shrugged then sighed a bit. "Bliss is sweet. If I didn't know she had my brother so wrapped around her finger, I'd worry about her. The women in our family aren't sweet. If this was Phoenix's wedding, I'd need a whole bottle of whiskey. But Bliss isn't Bridezilla. Which is a relief. I just don't like getting all dressed up and taking pictures, and having to let my mom fuss over my hair, and wearing all this makeup."

Maybe it was the whiskey, but I smirked at her rambling explanation. "You look hot as fuck. So there's that."

I don't think I'd ever told a female they looked hot as fuck. It was definitely the whiskey talking.

She broke into a grin then she laughed. It was a soft, surprised laugh and it was as intoxicating as her voice. "Eli Hardy, I do believe you're drunk."

I was pretty damn sure she was right, but she didn't know me well enough to make that assumption. "How so?" I asked with my own amused grin. She turned her body slightly toward me. The bench I'd taken as my own was under a large live oak tree and it was placed here for the wedding seeing as I'd never seen this bench at Bliss's parents before. It was just big enough for two people and when Ophelia turned to me, her shoulder brushed mine before her thigh made brief contact. Her scent wafted toward me with the breeze as if she'd coordinated with the weather. It wasn't the familiar floral scent most perfumes had, but it reminded me of coconut and sunshine. The best smells of summer radiating from her skin.

Whatever it was, I had the urge to bury my head in her neck and inhale deeply. But I wasn't that drunk.

"We've been in the same place a few times. I've watched you. I like to observe people," she explained with a small lift of her bare perfectly tanned left shoulder. "You're the good guy. The one everyone knows will do and say the right thing."

That snapped me out of whatever drunken attraction I'd been feeling toward her. I'd just thought the same damn thing, but I didn't need a female coming and rubbing it in my face. Why was I the good guy? Why did I do everything so damn straight and narrow? A memory of the last time I'd gotten drunk and done something stupid came to me.

"I had a one-night stand, drunk and didn't remember it," I told her as if this was enough to make me a badass. It made me a dick. But what the hell ever.

She did that sexy laugh again and as much as I didn't want to soak in the sound of it and admire the sheer beauty of her face . . . that's what I did. Her lips were so damn full, could they even be real?

"I don't think the sexcapade you and Lila Kate had her first night in Sea Breeze makes you bad. We all know Lila Kate is the closest thing to a perfect angel there is and she wasn't drunk, just tipsy from the Jell-O shot you gave her." She sounded amused as she mentioned the shots I'd honestly forgotten about.

I paused a moment. "She told you about that?" I asked a little shocked.

"We *are* roommates. Although she's rarely home, but I have known her my entire life. Our mothers are best friends." She sighed. "Her wedding is the next one I'll have to be a part of," she said that a bit sourly.

"I heard she got engaged," I replied. It hadn't affected me. I'd been happy for her and kind of assumed that was a given from the start.

Ophelia nodded. "Yeah, I knew it was happening. They just

made it official. I'll have that big flat all to myself since Cruz bought them a house on the country club land. But another event where I have to get all dressed up and do this." She waved her hand in front of her as if this was the worst thing in the world she could be forced to endure.

"It could be worse. You could be the Bride's Best Man," I said jokingly. Because my role in this wedding was anything but traditional.

Ophelia laughed again and I liked how it felt to make her laugh. Those eyes of hers sure were something. "The fact you and Dad are the only two in the wedding party is the best thing about this. I don't have to stand up there while everyone stares at me. I'm not so lucky in Lila Kate's wedding." She rolled her eyes. "Maid of Honor in that one."

The fact Ophelia didn't want to be stared at intrigued me. She got stared at daily. She would get stared at in sweats and her hair in a ponytail. She was that kind of good looking.

"You should be used to getting stared at," I told her.

She frowned, her nose slightly scrunched and damn if it didn't make this sultry beauty look adorable. "Why?"

The sincerity in that question wasn't lost on me. Even slightly intoxicated I saw in her expressive eyes she was serious. There was no way in hell this woman didn't know she was gorgeous. Women who looked like this knew. She wasn't simply beautiful like Lila. Ophelia's physical appearance was on another realm of stunning. Lila was as beautiful inside as she was outside and that had made her so damn appealing.

Ophelia was the kind men got one look at and fantasized about over and over again. She didn't even have to speak. Just one look and you were memorizing that image for later.

"Because it's impossible for anyone to not want to look at you once they get a glimpse," I replied then took another drink although it was probably a bad idea to drink more.

"You might want to slow down there," Ophelia said and took the flask from my hand. "You've got to stand by the bride soon and not fall over. Bliss is sweet, but she may not forgive you passing out drunk at her wedding ceremony easily."

I let Ophelia take my flask without argument. She had a point. Plus that would give me a reason to talk to her later. I'd need to retrieve my flask. Maybe I could follow that up with asking her to dance. Just as my imagination started to take that thought and run, we were interrupted.

"How long has he been drunk?" Cruz Kerrington asked. Even in my intoxicated state, I could hear the amusement in his voice. Damn fucking Kerrington

"Not sure. He was already into the flask when I joined him," Ophelia replied. I squinted against the sun behind Kerrington's head. He was smirking.

I saw him shake his head once and then he laughed. "Damn if this shit ain't funny," he replied. Then he held out his hand to me and for a moment I thought he wanted to shake mine. I stared at it like he was the one who was drunk. Why the fuck would I want to shake his hand? I didn't like the bastard. Couldn't remember why but I didn't. That much I did know.

"The wedding is in an hour. You need some food in your stomach and a cold ass shower," Cruz said more firmly. When I still didn't move, he sighed. "Do you want Bliss to hate you? Because she's going to be furious and Nate will beat the hell out of you if you ruin this for her."

I started to argue that Nate Finlay wasn't man enough to beat the hell out of me but stopped. Because I wasn't so sure that was the point right now. Cruz was a bastard, but he was right about Bliss hating me if I ruined this day for her. I didn't take Cruz's extended hand, but I did stand up. Staggered a little to the left before Cruz caught me from falling on my face.

"Do you think you can sober him up in time?" Ophelia asked from somewhere behind me. I wanted to turn around and look at her again, but all my focus needed to be on standing up straight.

"I may fuck up a lot of shit but this I'm the master of," Cruz said with pride in his voice. I rolled my eyes. What did Lila see in this arrogant dickhead? Oh wait . . . he was a bad boy. They all wanted a bad boy. Every damn one of them. If he didn't do bad boy shit, then they weren't interested. Give a girl a guy who makes all the wrong decisions and she's sunk.

"That I believe," Ophelia replied to Cruz. This time I had my balance, so I turned to look at her one more time.

"Next time I'll buy you a whiskey," I told her. Not sure if that was a good thing or not.

She smiled and bit her lip although her eyes appeared to be laughing at me. "I'll remember that," she replied.

"Fuck he needs food. Come on lover boy. You do not need to go flirting with a Finlay," Cruz said and jerked my arm in the direction of the house.

"Why?" I asked trying to free myself from his hold but only managing to stumble along beside him instead.

"They'll eat you up. You're too damn soft."

I didn't like being called soft. "I'm not fucking soft." I jerked free this time as I said it and just managed to keep from falling back on my ass.

Cruz groaned in frustration. "Fine, you're a tough son of a bitch. Now come on. We are wasting time."

Before I could tell him I didn't need his help, Bliss appeared on the front porch all dressed in white and looking like the angel I always knew she was. Pausing, I watched as she beamed at her mother who joined her. This was her big day. The one she'd once thought she may never see.

*"What if I don't grow up . . . what if I don't fall in love and get
married?" Her voice was weak from the chemo treatments and her head
now completely bald. Still, I'd never seen anyone as beautiful as Bliss.*

*"You will. You'll get your wedding. With the princess dress, the
sunshine, your family and friends, and a guy who will love you forever."
I said the words fiercely because they had to be true. A life without Bliss
in it wasn't possible.*

*Her smile was soft and her skin so pale it scared me. "Promise me,
Eli?" she asked.*

"I swear it," I replied.

That memory sobered me better than anything Cruz Kerrington had in mind. I took in the scene and silently thanked a
God I wasn't sure existed. But I had pleaded with him so many
times for years while Bliss battled leukemia that if He was there,
then He needed to be thanked for listening.

"I need coffee," I finally said to Cruz.

"Fuck yeah you do," he replied.

I fell into step beside him and we made our way to the side
door of the house that led into the kitchen. There was a flurry
going on with preparations for the reception. Cruz ignored the
lady who told him to get out and took a couple small sandwiches
off the tray she was preparing.

"This is the bride's best man. He needs food and coffee to
soak up the damn whiskey," Cruz said to the younger girl who
looked to be swooning over him instead of scolding him.

The girl got to work on my coffee and Cruz moved me toward the hallway.

My sister Crimson stepped out of Bliss's old bedroom about
that time and her eyes locked on me. I saw the realization as she
took in my appearance. If only she could have been my youngest

sister Cleo. Why in fuck's sake did I have to see Crimson right at this moment?

"Jesus, Eli, seriously!" she hissed. "You look like shit. This is Bliss's wedding day and you're drunk in the middle of the afternoon. How could you? This isn't like you? Is this about . . ." she paused and looked at Cruz who was standing silently beside me. Instead of handing me a sandwich he shoved one in my mouth.

"He's sobering up now. I got this. Go find someone else to bitch at," Cruz said to Crimson. Her face turned bright red as she glared at him. I chewed quickly and swallowed. I had to handle this now before my sister said anything else. She was no match for Cruz and if he said anything mean to her, I'd have to kick his ass. In my current condition, I doubted I'd succeed.

Before I could swallow the food, Crimson spun on her heel and stormed away. Without another word. I was pretty fucking positive that had never happened in my life.

When the food was finally down, I asked, "How did you do that?"

Cruz frowned. "What?"

I pointed at my sister's retreating form.

He gave a dismissive shrug. "I just told her it was handled."

I shook my head. "No, that's not what I mean. Crimson doesn't listen like that. At least to me or about me."

"She's younger than you, correct?" Cruz asked.

I nodded. But she was still bossy as hell.

Cruz ran a hand over his head and let out a sigh. "Damn. I don't think I've ever met a guy as fucking nice as you are. Shake that shit off, dude. Get a backbone. Be firm. Make your own decisions. You need to go and live. A fucking lot. Enjoy being your own man. Doing whatever the hell you want to do. Stop being so damn nice."

The way he said it made me feel like a loser. As if I had been living in a bubble afraid to see the world. "Just because I'm not a bastard doesn't mean I'm weak," I argued. "What about Lila? She deserves more from you than all that shit. She needs a man who will be there for her, love her, support her. Not some man who wants to call the shots and live some wild life." Yet she'd chosen this joker over me.

Cruz nodded. "I'm not talking about me. I know what's out there. I lived it. Then I accepted I'd been in love with Lila most of my life and she was what made me complete." he paused and pointed at me. "But you've not lived for shit. You have no idea what you want. And no woman will ever make you happy until you can appreciate her. Living life and making wrong choices makes it easier to know when you find what's right."

I opened my mouth to argue when he shoved another sandwich inside and I was forced to chew while I scowled at him. He studied me a moment then gave a nod like he had made a decision.

"You're lost, Eli Hardy. Motherfucking lost. Six months ago, I wouldn't have given a flying fuck. But I'm a different man now. So, when this wedding is over, you're gonna take the keys to my Harley and go. Just fucking go. Don't stop until you figure out what it is in life you want or where you belong. Just drive the damn thing. Make bad decisions. Get a tattoo, date a stripper, work in a bar."

There were a lot of things I could say at that moment. Several thoughts ran through my head. But in the end, I simply nodded.

This may be the biggest mistake of my life, but at least I was making it.

Chapter One

♥ OPHELIA FINLAY ♥

MAY 20 / 7:03 AM

THE COOL SPRING mornings were now gone. I missed those. Sitting outside with my coffee enjoying the sounds of the day was so peaceful. Now, the heat was back and nothing about sitting outside with early morning mosquitos and humidity was fun. Frowning, I stood at the large windows of the flat I lived in over the dance studio owned by my best friend, Lila Kate Kerrington. The parking lot was empty now, but in a couple of hours, it would be a busy Monday. The silence of living alone would have been hard to adjust to after Lila Kate had married and officially moved out six months ago, but the truth was she'd been sleeping at the house Cruz Kerrington had bought them for the most part anyway.

I didn't mind the solitude. I was thankful Lila Kate had agreed to let me lease the place on my own. I loved the location and I still had no idea what I wanted to do with my life. I hadn't gone back to college after my break. The fact I was turning twenty-two in a few months made that a little stressful if I thought about it too much. Instead I pretended like working at the dance studio was exactly what I wanted to do. I liked my job well enough. I got to work for Lila Kate and that was always fun. Maybe answering the phones, updating the website, stocking the dance store, and handling the class schedules wasn't an ideal forever career for me but it worked for now.

Besides, it wasn't like I had a dream to chase. Even as I thought it, the corners of my mouth sank. Why did that bother me so badly? Not having a dream. I should be glad I wasn't chasing something. Fighting daily to achieve some out of reach goal. I was content.

I drank down the last of my coffee in one big gulp and ignored the knot in my chest that didn't agree with me. It was an annoying little knot. Always creeping up when I didn't want it around. Life was good here. No need for me to get restless.

My phone rang and for once I was thankful for the distraction of a call. Normally I stared at it in horror until it ended. My voice mail message would tell them to text me. Which was my preferred communication. I had to answer the calls in the studio all day. I didn't want to do it in my personal life too.

My sister-in-law's name appeared on the screen. Bliss was one of the few people who rarely attempted to call me. She knew I liked to text and always did that instead of calling. Not to mention it was early. Snatching the phone up immediately concerned, I quickly said, "Bliss, hey, everything okay?"

"Yes." Her voice sounded amused. I instantly relaxed. "I didn't mean to scare you. Sorry. I'm just driving and couldn't text. I knew you'd be awake getting ready for work, so I figured calling was safe," she explained.

"Of course. What's up?" I replied.

"I wanted to see if you were busy this weekend. The house is finally finished with the renovations and the new and improved pool is complete. Anyway, we were going to have a party to celebrate originally, but the Hardys received some bad news last week. Eli's grandmother is undergoing surgery this weekend and we decided to have everyone over Friday night as more of a support of friends. Everyone needs something to get their mind off of it all. We would love to have you here, to see the house and us."

Sea Breeze, Alabama was only a two-hour drive away, but I hadn't been to visit my brother and his wife there in months. They'd been here to visit several times and I'd not found a reason to go back. I had been back only once since their wedding last summer. It was time to visit and getting out of my routine here would do me some good. Maybe the restlessness I had begun to battle lately would ease if I took a little short trip.

I told her, "I'll be there."

"Wonderful! I can't wait to see you. Come whenever you can get away. I'll have the guestroom overlooking the gulf ready for you."

"I'll talk to Lila Kate. We normally don't have late Friday classes. She does some private classes, but I'm not needed in the afternoon for long. I should be able to leave here by three Friday at the latest," I told her.

"I can't wait to see you. If you hear from Phoenix, tell her I'm trying to get in touch with her too. But her phone number is saying it's not working . . ." Bliss trailed off as if she wasn't sure if she'd said the right thing or not. My younger sister was a hellion and getting worse with each year. I hadn't heard from her in three weeks since she showed up here drunk and needed to sleep it off before going to see our parents the next day. How she hadn't flunked out of college yet, I had no idea. But the phone thing was odd.

"How long has it been giving you that message?" I asked, knowing Mom called to check on Phoenix daily. She needed the reassurance her baby was still alive. My poor momma.

"I called her three times before calling you. I was trying to catch her before she was in class."

I held back a laugh. Phoenix had no early morning classes. The girl couldn't get up before mid-morning at the earliest. "I'll tell her. See you Friday," I told Bliss before ending the call. I quickly found my sister's name and hit call. Waited . . . and sure enough, the not a working number message played in my ear. Frowning, I looked at my phone and tried to think of every possible scenario. My parents paid her phone bill. She was a college student. They covered those things while we went to college. When I had decided to take a "break" from college, they'd agreed and would have kept paying my bills if I hadn't asked for them to be handed over.

Knowing there had to be a reasonable explanation, I started to call my mother and stopped. Just in case there was something going on that would upset her, I decided calling Dad was a better idea. Mom was tough, but when it came to her baby girl, she got very worked up. It wasn't that she loved Phoenix more, it was that she feared for Phoenix more. My sister was crazy as hell. With a mean streak a mile wide.

"Morning, beautiful," my dad's voice said over the line after the first ring.

"Good morning, Daddy," I replied.

"I rarely ever get calls from you. Is it just my lucky day?" he was teasing. I visited my parents regularly. I also texted both of them. I did call my mom more though. The older I got, the worse that got. Needing to talk to her about things.

"I was wondering if you had heard from Phoenix?" I asked, getting to the point before my imagination got the best of me.

"Yes, I spoke with her yesterday. Why? Did she call you?"

Yesterday? That's weird. "So yesterday her phone number was working?"

He paused. "It was . . . but as of today, it won't be." He knew about this, which meant she was okay.

"I tried calling her." I stopped and waited for him to explain.

There was a heavy sigh then he cleared his throat. "Phoenix has decided she's in love with a guy she met on her recent trip to London. She's not taking her exams and finishing up this semester of college even though the tests are this week. Tossing it away because she doesn't want to leave him. It's her choice, but after speaking with your mother, we decided that if she can so easily toss away the money we have spent this semester on her college education with no regard to her future, it's time we take a more firm hand. She wants to be grown and make her own decisions then she can. Starting with paying her own bills."

Oh.

Shit.

I sat there with the phone in my hand unable to find words. Phoenix was in London with some man and our parents had cut her off financially. I was torn between being furious with her stupidity and panicking over her safety. She couldn't survive out there. My little sister made the worst choices on a good day. Sure, not too long ago I'd been wild. Made some bad decisions. Was a little rebellious but it was a phase. I did "take a break" from college and not return but otherwise, I was doing good now. I'd never have run off to freaking London no matter how bad I got.

"How's Mom?" I asked finally.

"Worried but like me, she knows we can't keep funding Phoenix's bad decisions. She has to grow up. Or at least step up and learn how to handle life on her own."

They were right, but she wasn't ready. The idea of getting on a plane and going to find her and slap sense into her was tempting.

But so was finding her and holding her tight so she couldn't do anything stupid that could hurt her.

"You haven't told Nate," I said, already knowing the answer since it was Bliss who called me about the number.

"No. I was putting it off. He's finished the renovations on the house and they're enjoying things being done there. No need to put a damper on things for him."

Nate would freak the hell out when he heard this. Damper was a very tame way to describe his reaction. Dad knew that too.

"Bliss called Phoenix this morning. She's who called me to ask about the not a working number message."

Another sigh. "She's supposed to call with her new London number by noon. I'll make sure you get it then I'll call and deal with your brother."

"Okay," I said, wanting to ask him more questions. Like did he have an address for her and had he done a background check on the guy or call some connection in London to find out more. But I didn't.

Instead, I ended the call with our usual "bye love you" and hung up.

Sinking into the kitchen chair, I stared out the window no longer enjoying the view.

Chapter Two

~ELI HARDY~

MAY 23 / 9:10 PM

*W*HEN I'D DRIVEN away from this town a year ago, I hadn't planned on being gone so long, but until a call I got from my dad last week, I hadn't even thought about returning. Life had changed me. They would never understand just how much. No one would and I wasn't ready to tell anyone why or how. I had dealt with the demons and they hadn't destroyed me. But there were times I thought little reminders just might.

Returning to Sea Breeze wasn't what I was ready to do. Finding a way to face each day the past six months had been hard enough. Seeing my family wasn't what I wanted to do and my life would never be here again. Even though it had been an easier life I left behind in Sea Breeze. Memories from that part of my life didn't hurt anymore. Pain had been something I hadn't truly experienced then. I'd been a spoiled fool thinking the events that had taken place back then were real heartbreaks. No love I'd experienced in Sea Breeze had ever brought me to my knees. That power was solely given to losing a life . . . beauty . . . innocence that in the end had never truly been real. A façade that would forever haunt me.

In the morning, I'd go to my parents' house. They were expecting me. I was sure my sisters would be there. My aunt Larissa, her husband Micah Falco, and her daughter Jilly. There was a good chance my aunt Amanda, Uncle Preston and their three sons would be there too. The family would come together. They'd support each other as they always did.

Our gran was well loved. My father's mother was our only grandmother. She was either a saint or an angel. Not many women would raise a child as her own that had been abandoned by her husband's mistress. I was too young to remember it all, but Larissa had been the result of an affair my granddad had before I was born. Larissa's mother had taken off even after my granddad had left my grandmother to live with the other woman and raise Larissa.

All that was history now. Something all of us forgot about, even Larissa. Gran was her mother. She saw it no other way. She adored her, and I knew that she would be taking this news the hardest.

Gran had been diagnosed with colon cancer. Surgery was scheduled two days from now. We would know then if and where it had spread. I inhaled deeply as the memory of my dad's voice cracking as he told me over the phone. I'd never seen my dad cry or breakdown. But he'd been about to as the words came out of his mouth. My chest tightened again at the thought. My own emotions still raw from life and the knowledge of our fragile existence. My dad's tears didn't make him weak. It took a strong man to face the reality of death and loss. To embrace the emotions and be able to weep.

Life didn't play favorites or keep score. It didn't care about the innocent. If it did, my life would be very different now. The darkness inside me wouldn't exist. I would still know how to truly smile. If life cared at all, babies wouldn't die and my gran would live forever because of the beauty of her soul. She'd given more love than anyone I had ever known. She was the reason I believed in forgiveness. Even if I knew I'd never truly be able to forgive. I wasn't like my gran. If life cared, it would take me instead.

I climbed off my bike and unhooked the duffle bag strapped on the back before turning to look at the house in front of me. It was impressive. Bliss had mentioned renovations they were doing to the already nice beachfront home they lived in a few months back in a text message. Bliss was settled down now. Her role as my best friend had changed the moment she said "I do" and I knew that was one of the reasons I'd taken Cruz Kerrington's Harley and headed west with nothing but a change of clothes and a flask of whiskey.

I hadn't wanted to be here when it all changed. At least that's what I thought. I couldn't say I'd do it again if I had known what would unfold. The guy I once was seemed like another lifetime ago. He had thought he was lost and needing to find himself. What a load of shit. I had been clueless as to what real loss was.

Standing here knowing Bliss was inside with her husband didn't bother me at all. Which was why I had chosen to come here. I needed one night of sleep before facing my family. Before accepting the fact my gran might not be okay. Before my mother looked into my eyes and saw the emptiness that was unavoidable. She'd ask questions and I'd give her lies. The truth wasn't something I wanted to share. Not even to her.

Walking toward the house, I hadn't even made it to the front steps when the door swung open and Bliss came walking outside. Once upon a time, the sight of her long dark hair and blue eyes would grab me in the chest so tight I would lose my breath. Seeing her now, in the moonlight, I felt none of that. What was there was forever gone. Her presence didn't feel like home. Not anymore. Seeing the happy glow on her face told me she was happy. Her life had turned out the way she hoped. This was where she fit. If I wasn't hollow, I was sure that would give me peace. Nate Finlay had been her happily ever after even before she knew his name. Their lives had been intertwined since they were kids. I didn't begrudge her this obvious joy she'd found. I knew she had seen the darkness at a young age and fought it. Life had let her live. For that I was thankful.

"Is this real? Has my life long best friend returned and . . ." she paused as she slowly took in my changes once I stepped into the light from the house floodlights. Her eyes went wide and her jaw dropped. I forgot how much my appearance had changed but seeing the shock in Bliss's eyes I realized this was going to happen a lot over the next few days. I should warn my dad so he could prepare my mother. "Holy . . . Oh . . ."

A loud bark of masculine laughter followed by, "Holy fuck, man," came from Nate as he stepped out onto the porch to stand beside Bliss.

"Eli Hardy," Bliss said slowly as if she needed to reassure herself this was in fact me. I wanted to say, "No. He won't ever return. Because he wouldn't. He was gone." The man I was now was permanently altered inside much more so than outside. "Has your mother seen you yet?"

That got another laugh from Nate but Bliss ignored him and her eyes scanned my tattoos and hair. I didn't want her to look into my eyes. If anyone could see the change, she would. She knew the boy I had been too well. I didn't step farther into the light. I kept the shadows over my face enough to mask the rest.

"No. Came here first. I need a night of sleep before I face everyone . . . and deal with things," I finally replied. I had to speak if I intended to stay at their house.

My words reminded her of why I was here. I saw the shadow of understanding and fear cross her face. Bliss understood cancer all too well. She was a survivor. "I'm so sorry," she said the words I knew I'd hear a lot. Coming from her I knew she meant them. They weren't just words because she didn't know what else to say. She knew the horror of the disease. She'd faced death and lived.

I gave a nod. There was no reason to say anything. I'd been by her side as a teenager while she fought to live. I'd seen it even if I hadn't experienced it. I had thought I understood death and the fear that came with it. But what I had experienced at Bliss's side as a kid was nothing compared to what I knew now. Dying isn't the part to fear. It's surviving.

"Eli, if your mother doesn't already know about this," she motioned toward me. "The changes in your appearance. I think," she paused and took a deep breath. "Maybe she needs to be warned before you walk into her house with all your family there." I could tell Bliss didn't want to say this to me, but she thought it needed to be said.

"Normally I'd say to hell with it but she's right under the circumstances," Nate added but he was still grinning in amusement and possibly there was some respect in his eyes. For what? The ink on my body? It wasn't something to respect. It was reminders of what I would never forget.

"I mean no one has seen you in over a year. There was no warning. I hadn't thought that goodbye hug you gave me before we left on our honeymoon was a literal goodbye." There was hurt in Bliss's tone. Once that would have made me feel guilty. As if I should apologize. If I could find that reaction, then there would be a possibility of hope I'd kept a piece of me through it all. After six months, I already knew it was an impossibility. Even for my childhood best friend. No emotion came.

"Can I get a shower and borrow a bed for the night?" I asked instead of reassuring her I'd tell my parents. I didn't reassure anymore. Reassurance was a waste of breath. Something we did because we thought it was a necessity.

She frowned and then nodded. "Of course. Come on inside." She stepped back, and Nate wrapped an arm around her waist loosely. It seemed like some sort of comfort thing. If I had upset her, I knew he would reassure her. I walked by them and into the house. Vaulted tongue and groove ceilings, wide open space, money. Wealth. Taken for granted. Not because they were selfish but because they'd known nothing else. I'd been just like them once.

"Are you hungry? Or thirsty?" Bliss asked from behind me. I finished scanning all they'd done before turning to look at them.

"A beer would be good," I replied. "Place looks great, but then it was nice before."

"It's taken almost a year, but it's exactly what we wanted. Dealing with contractors was a bitch. But other than that, it's not been bad."

"Heineken or we have some from the new microbrewery in town," Bliss said from the fridge.

"The local stuff isn't bad," Nate added.

"I'll try the local then," I replied. I didn't give a shit what it was, but the response would cause Bliss to look too closely. Ask things I wouldn't answer.

"Are you hungry? I could heat up the leftovers from dinner. Blackened shrimp pasta," she added.

I was too tired for food. "No thanks. I'm good."

Bliss didn't look convinced but walked back over to me with an open bottle of beer. I took it and noticed her staring at my right arm that was covered in tattoos. I could tell she was trying to figure out what they were. Why they were there.

"When did you decide to get addicted to ink?" Nate asked as

he sank down on the large white leather sectional sofa closest to where we were standing. I shrugged and took a long pull from the beer.

After I swallowed and walked over to an extra wide blue chair across from the sofa, dropped my duffle bag to the floor beside it then sat down before replying, "Wasn't a decision. Just happened."

"How exactly does"—Bliss waved a hand at me as she sat down beside her husband—"that just happen?"

It didn't just fucking happen. There was a reason, but those reasons were mine. She seemed annoyed. Because I wasn't the guy she once knew? Or because she disapproved of the new me? I didn't care. Pleasing Bliss no longer mattered to me. I wanted her happy and she was. That was clear. Wasn't my job to please her now just as it hadn't been then. I had wanted it to be once. Knowing deep down it never would be. It all seemed shallow to think I'd once weighed my happiness on her.

"It just happens," I replied with no intention of saying more.

She then waggled her finger in the direction of my hair. "I've never seen it so long," she was going to keep on until she was satisfied with an answer.

I just nodded. She was right. I'd never let it grow out like this before.

"Up the stairs and the first door on the left is a guest bedroom. It has its own bathroom. You'll see the towels when you walk in to our right. Make yourself at home," Nate said before Bliss could ask me more questions I wasn't going to answer.

"Thanks," I told him and stood back up. "I appreciate y'all letting me crash here tonight."

"You're always welcome here," Nate told me, and I watched as his hand rested on Bliss's knee. He was silently telling her to let me go. Nate was more perceptive than I'd given him credit for.

"If you want to go run in the morning, use the French doors.

They won't ding throughout the house when opened."

I hadn't gone for a run in six months.

"I don't run anymore. Goodnight," I said. I didn't wait on a response from Bliss. I took my duffle bag and headed for the staircase to the far right of the large open area.

I felt my phone vibrate in my pocket but ignored it. There was no one I wanted to talk to tonight. That would all have to wait until tomorrow. I knew without looking it was family. I'd gotten through all the questions I could handle for the moment.

Chapter Three

♥ OPHELIA FINLAY ♥

MAY 24 / 6:45 PM

MY PLAN TO leave at three hadn't gone accordingly. I'd gotten my things packed, cleaned up the flat, taken out all the trash, then when I finally got into my car, the change engine oil light came on. I was never good about remembering to get my oil changed. Glancing up at the sticker in the far left corner of my window I realized I was three thousand miles over-due. Dang it!

There had been a wait at the Lube Express and it had taken them almost an hour to get my car serviced. By that time, I was starving and went to grab a chicken wrap to take with me, but again there were people. So many people. It was the time of year that Fridays got busy in Rosemary Beach. Vacationers arriving for their week at the beach. Nothing was fast or easy for the next three months.

After getting some food and heading toward Sea Breeze, it

was almost five and I called to let Bliss know I was running late yet again and would just be arriving in time for the party or whatever it was. I didn't think party was a good description. Not under the circumstances. The mention of Eli Hardy had reminded me of Bliss and Nate's wedding. We had drunk some whiskey from his flask together and talked briefly.

Eli wasn't my type, but he'd been drunk, so he had been more laid back. It had made me see a side of him I did like. But I doubted that side ever came out when he was sober. Eli was way too uptight. I liked more adventure. Not the bad boys but the ones with an edge. Eli was just too good. When he'd left the wedding on Cruz Kerrington's bike, I'd been impressed, but that was honestly the last time I'd thought about him until Bliss had mentioned him earlier this week. Now I wondered what had come of him after the wedding. I did know Cruz no longer had the bike. Lila Kate had mentioned her relief that he'd sold it a few weeks after the wedding, but she had been surprised Eli had been who bought it.

My thoughts went from Eli to my sister, and then I worried over Phoenix's bad choices. Dad had texted me her phone number like he promised. I had called her three times this week and all she ever did was text me a response. The last had been "Not your business!!!" so I had backed off and let her be. I couldn't force Phoenix to talk to me. However, my thoughts stayed on her the rest of the drive. By the time I pulled in front of Nate and Bliss's house, it was full of cars outside. Lights spilled from every window and I took a moment to take in the beautiful place my brother now called home. He'd start a family here. One day I'd visit and there would be kids calling me Aunt Ophelia. Bliss couldn't get pregnant, but they already talked about adopting in the future. My chest felt warm at the thought of all that would one day come for them.

Then just as quickly, I felt the melancholy follow because I didn't think I'd ever know their happiness. I'd dated enough men to realize what they had was rare. Every time I thought maybe I'd found someone, it turned bad. He wasn't what he'd led me to believe. He changed. Maybe it was me that made them change. It had happened so many times now I was willing to take some blame for it. Obviously, I was the common denominator.

Deep down I feared my appearance attracted them, but once they truly knew me, they were turned away. I was facing the fact I must be flawed. There was something about my personality that men thought they could take me for granted, treat me poorly, and then become disinterested.

I wasn't a Bliss, and I wasn't a Lila Kate. Both of those two had the beauty along with the sweet goodness. They were beautiful souls. Men were drawn to them. Loved them. Adored them. Women like them were the ones who got the happily ever after.

I thought some days I was fine doing life on my own. I didn't have to worry about anyone else. Just do what I wanted and make my own decisions. It sounded like a solid plan. One that would make me happy and content. That only lasted for awhile though.

When you've been raised by two people who love each other as fiercely as my parents do, who fight then make up, who laugh together, work through all obstacles together, it's hard not to want that. It was all we saw as kids and even now they still complete each other. Living in a home like that was the one thing making me wish for more. They were the reason I said yes to a date when I knew deep down it would end the same as all the others.

Everyone said I was so much like my mother. But I knew it was in looks only. I looked like a young Blaire Finlay and that was where it ended. My mother was everything I ever wanted to be, but I knew I never would be. Her beauty was deep, her love was strong, her will was more than I could comprehend. She'd battled so much early in life and came out on top. I had decided that was the difference. I'd had no battles.

My family life had been storybook perfect. I had wanted for nothing. I'd been given all the love, security, and support a child could be given. Nate was a man, so maybe that's how it affected him differently. He learned to be the man our father was by living the life we'd had. But Phoenix was as messed up as I was. Her flaws were different. But we both struggled in our own ways. I wouldn't trade my family and the life they'd given me for the world, but I feared it had kept me from having any real grit. There was nothing about me of real worth.

The door to the house opened and I saw my brother who looked as much like our father as I did our mother, step out onto the front step. It was a good distance from where I had parked but even from here, I knew his gaze was locked on me. He'd been waiting for me. That made me smile. Always the big brother.

I grabbed my Louis Vuitton duffle bag. It was all I had packed for such a short visit and climbed out of my Audi to go meet him before he walked all the way out here. He waited where he was when he saw me headed for the house finally. I wondered if he had seen me drive up and had been waiting on me to come inside. I wasn't sure how long I had sat there lost in my thoughts. Unfortunately, they were thoughts I got lost in a lot lately.

It had been over a year since my last relationship. For awhile, I was good with being single, but I realized I was lonely. Phoenix and I hadn't been close in years and especially now that she'd run off. Lila Kate was married and living her life as Mrs. Cruz Kerrington now. I didn't really have any female friends. I'd never liked other females. I tried growing up, but I always ended up with the boys. Girls were too dramatic. They were so competitive. I just couldn't take the constant fighting that seemed to break out all the time.

"I was about to come looking for you," Nate said as I reached the top stair. He held out his arms and I stepped into them to return the hug. "Missed you, sis," he said.

All my other worries and concerns melted. I was here at his house where he had found his happy. And that made everything right in the world. "I missed you too," I told him.

He took my duffle bag as he stepped back. "I'll take this to your room. Bliss took a hell of a long time up there making sure it was ready for you. I think she even put some fucking fresh flowers by the bed. Say something about them, will you."

I smiled at that. He reminded me so much of Dad. I nodded. "I'm not a complete bitch, you know. I would have thanked her without you telling me."

He smirked. "No, you're not a bitch. Our baby sister gets that title hands down."

We had always made jokes about Phoenix and her redheaded personality. It was all in fun, but I wondered if he knew about her current stupid move. I decided I'd talk to him about it later. Not now. He had a house full of people. Those who had become his friends and family once he fell in love with and married Bliss.

I'd always thought our parents' circle of friends and their families was abnormally large, but Bliss and her circle was even bigger. They were also much closer. It was overwhelming when they were all together. I'd experienced it at their engagement party, Bliss's birthday party, and the wedding. Now I was back for more.

I started to walk inside when Nate said, "Just a head's up. There's a bit of tension in there. They are all acting like it's not, but you'll notice. Don't ask about Eli."

I paused. "Eli's not here?" That seemed very unlike Eli. He was responsible and being at a gathering at his best friend's house with his family the night before his grandmother's surgery seemed like a big deal.

Nate sighed, but the scowl on his face was clear. He was pissed and trying to hide it. What the heck was going on?

"He came here last night. First time anyone had seen him since the wedding. He left early to go to his grandparents' house. His dad had called and said they were all having breakfast there as a family. Apparently, he left there after breakfast and no one has seen him since."

"Eli?" I asked again still having a hard time associating Eli with the description I was getting.

Nate nodded. "He's changed. In a lot of ways. Even Bliss doesn't understand him."

The front door opened again, and Micah Falco stepped outside. He looked from Nate with an annoyed glance as if the party inside was too much for him then turned to me with a tight smile. "Hey," he said then held up a cigar. "Beer isn't enough for this bullshit. I need this or I'm breaking into the motherfucking whiskey."

Nate nodded. "Understood. Just make sure you smoke it far enough away from the house that Bliss can't smell it inside."

"I will." He held out his hand toward me. "You're Ophelia, correct?"

I shook his hand. "Yes, and you're Micah, Larissa's husband."

He grinned then. "Yeah. I knew we'd met before but it's always at celebration events and I've had one too many."

I'd seen him drunk more than I'd seen him sober. I smiled politely and gave a nod.

"If that motherfucker don't get his ass here soon, Larissa may wish I'd had one too many. I'm ready to beat his sorry tattooed ass." He walked off then down the stairs and toward the beach. Nate didn't seem confused by that last sentence, but I was. Who else was he expecting to show up? I thought Eli not being here was the issue. But he'd said something about tattoos.

Eli Hardy did not have tattoos. The idea of Eli with tattoos made me smile. It was that out of character for him. Someone else must be missing. Maybe Eli had brought a friend?

Nate motioned for me to go inside and I was about to ask about the other missing guest when Bliss appeared at the door looking as perfectly polished as always. Her smile softened when she saw me and again, I was being embraced. I returned her hug.

"Sorry I'm so late," I said, thinking it was probably better that I was since there was family drama I was not a part of going on.

"Be glad you are," she whispered then stepped back. "Nate has your bag. Good. He can take it to your room, and I'll get you something to drink. You need it tonight. Trust me."

I followed her toward the kitchen and as much as I wanted to take in the place now they had redone it I didn't want anyone to think I was staring at them. The place was covered with folks. Bliss stepped up to the marble bar and glanced back at me. "Champagne, wine, or stronger?"

I took one quick peek at the room and then replied "stronger."

Chapter Four

~ELI HARDY~

MAY 24 / 8:36 PM

WALKING INSIDE MEANT facing bullshit from everyone. Not showing up at all meant bullshit from everyone. Fuck this.

I climbed off my bike and ran a hand through my hair. I hadn't planned on being late. But I didn't plan much. I'd had to get away from it all after this morning. The fear that was clear on everyone's face despite their smiles and false cheer had just reminded me of the reality. Facts I knew by looking at them that Dad hadn't told me. It was bad. They already knew how bad but they weren't saying.

The only one who hadn't been shocked or horrified by my tattoos, long hair, and absence was my gran. She'd laughed and clapped her hands in delight when she saw me. Told me her beautiful boy was even more decorated now. When anyone mentioned my being gone, she would jump in with a comment about me being brave enough to live, or finding a life out there. That shut them up real damn fast. I'd found life, alright and I knew now that it was cold, harsh and unforgiving.

I said very little. Listening to Gran talk, memorizing her face when she smiled, soaking in the sound of her laughter. Things that could be taken and never returned were what I would lock away. Keep close. I wasn't naïve enough to think I'd have Gran forever. Even if she survived this, time would still pass, age would still come. We weren't given infinite time on earth.

Drinking all day at a bar just past the Florida/Alabama line was probably not the best way to spend the rest of my day. But fuck if I cared about what was the best way. It was the way I handled it all. I didn't move toward the house. Instead I scanned the cars parked outside. Might as well know who was still here.

Gran wasn't. I knew that without looking. She'd be in bed by now. Tomorrow morning would come too soon.

My parents were here and so were my sisters Crimson and Cleo. Cage and Eva York were and at least two of their three sons. Preston and Amanda Drake were here, and I wasn't sure what their sons drove, but they were always with the York boys. Good chance they would be inside too. Dewayne and Siena Falco. My aunt Larissa would be here with her husband, Micah Falco. Looked like a few of the Taylors were here too. I didn't see Saffron or Holland Corbin's vehicles and thank fuck for that.

After another moment of debating if going in there was worth it, I took the first step in that direction. I stunk of cigarettes even though I didn't smoke, and whiskey. That I did consume plenty of. I was sure I looked like I'd had a fifth.

"You really going in there looking like that?" The thick southern drawl that reminded me of fucking honey every time I heard it stopped me. I turned my gaze toward the voice. I had forgotten how she sounded until she'd spoken. The memory of the last time

I'd seen her wasn't clear, but it hadn't faded either.

Ophelia Finlay stepped out of the shadows with a glass of something dark in her glass. The long blonde hair of hers appeared platinum under the moonlight and those eyes that could draw in any man twinkled up at me with mischief. She was stunning. Possibly the most beautiful woman I'd ever seen. Not that it mattered. Beauty was fleeting, it was evil, it was powerful. It could destroy a man. However, I was safe with this one. My destruction had already come.

"They're all pissed at you. I thought it was the not being here thing, but I see now what Micah was referring to when he mentioned 'tattoos.' If I wasn't seeing this with my own eyes, I don't think I'd believe it."

She wasn't one of "them" . . . my family . . . my friends . . . someone I needed to hide from. I moved closer toward her. I could stall. Going inside was expected by everyone, except her. She wouldn't care. "You think they're pissed over my tattoos?" I asked her, not caring what her response was. Just that I had more seconds not to face the others.

She lifted a bare tanned shoulder. The top she was wearing was strapless. Her tits doing an excellent job of holding the top up on their own. A strand of her hair that looked like silk fell over her skin. "I'm sure your disappearing act today and no show tonight might play a big part," she said then tilted her head to the side slightly. Her bluish-silver eyes slanting. "Eli Hardy, have you gone bad?" There was a teasing lilt to her voice but there was also an interest that I didn't miss. She hadn't been interested in the man I once was but the damaged one before her was appealing. What the fuck was wrong with women?

Showing her how "bad" I'd gone was so fucking tempting. The image of Ophelia Finlay naked pressed against me was a damn fantasy I had to stay clear of. She was attached to a life I no longer belonged to.

"Not the same guy," I replied.

She took another step toward me and the way her hips swayed with the movement would tempt any man. Even one as disillusioned as me.

She reached out a hand and one bright pink nail barely grazed my ink covering my right bicep. "It's beautiful," she said breathlessly. "You chose a talented artist."

This wasn't something new for me. Women were drawn to the tattoos. I hadn't realized it or cared when I'd walked into the shop to get my first one. I wondered if the man I had once been would have gotten ink if he'd known Ophelia Finlay would touch him this way. Flash her hypnotic gaze up at him and lower her already seductive voice as she spoke.

Yes. He would have. He'd have been owned by her so easily. The wildness in her eyes would have been exotic and fucking enticing. The man I was now, however, knew the games women played. He saw the lies in their eyes. He knew the manipulation they used as a weapon.

She tilted her head back to look up at me. Those eyes couldn't fuck with me. I was sure she was used to using them to control men, to sink them. Ophelia had met her match. "Is there more under your shirt? It looks like it's there." She then moved her hand to touch my neck. The smell of coconut wafted close. She still smelled like the summer. Her scent made you instantly long for the beach. Ophelia wasn't the kind of woman that should smell like something so warm and calming. Yet even with all I knew, how cold my blood ran, the scent of her drew me in for a moment. Made me want to taste her, feel her, explore her. All things better left alone.

Her finger ran under the collar of my t-shirt. "It looks like it covers your chest too." Her voice was thick and soft all at once. As if she didn't want anyone to hear us. She knew they were looking for me inside, but she was keeping me out here. To herself. I was in no hurry and although this would lead to nothing, I allowed it go on.

"It does. Not all of my chest. But some." My voice was deeper than normal. I sounded affected by her touch. Fuck, I was a man. Of course I was. My soul was dark, but my desire wasn't gone. I still had needs. I just didn't act on those needs anymore. I hadn't in a long time.

She didn't move closer, but it felt as if she did. There was no movement other than her gaze slowly traveling up my arm and neck until her eyes locked on mine. She didn't say anything. If she had, I wasn't sure I could have responded anyway. Ophelia was talented. She knew her allure and she used it like a fucking pro. That was dangerous for men and I had no doubt she'd broken many along the way. I studied her eyes, allowed myself to search their depths. For what I wasn't sure. Deceit, selfishness, or lust were all things I knew how to see now that I'd been blinded by them. The twisted thoughts I'd seen in another and been too naïve to understand weren't there in Ophelia's eyes. But then why would they be. She'd lived a life that didn't distort or tarnish. Her family had taught her love like mine had. I hoped she never got close to the other. Those who don't understand it are destroyed by it.

"You need to go inside," she said, breaking into my thoughts. I'd been silently standing over her trying to read her and she'd allowed it. Not once had she blinked or stepped away. I hadn't met a woman yet that stood so confident under that kind of blatant scrutiny. She stepped back and her hand fell from my chest where it had been resting. Even if she didn't realize it, she was closing the window she'd left open for me briefly. Almost as if she knew why I was looking and wanted to prove she had nothing to hide. That hadn't been the case, but it still felt like it.

They were waiting on me inside. I didn't have to go in there. My gran was gone on home for the night. I owed them nothing. But they were all hurting, and my presence was desired for whatever reason. They were family and that's what they did. The moonlight touched Ophelia's face again as she turned toward it. Beauty no longer affected me and although she was unarguably beautiful, there was something deeper that I saw. Maybe it was the carefree spirit I missed and wanted to be near. But leaving her out here was hard and it shouldn't be. Not just because I didn't want to be inside that house. There was more there under her skin. I would never know what it was because when I walked inside, I'd leave this all here. In the moment. Right now, standing this close to her, I was showing a weakness. Whatever voodoo Ophelia Finlay was weaving I was a willing participant. That would lead to nothing either of us wanted.

"It's good to see you again, Eli. Hopefully it won't be a year before the next time." She flashed me a pouty look as if the idea pained her. If I could still smile, I would. But not even Ophelia's voodoo was strong enough to change my past. She stepped around me to walk toward the house. I waited until she reached the top step before I took my eyes off her. The emptiness returned. Odd that I hadn't realized it had been gone. It was such a part of me that I would have thought I'd immediately recognized when it eased. I frowned at the door Ophelia had disappeared into. She wasn't a possibility I needed to entertain.

Chapter Five

♥ OPHELIA FINLAY ♥

MAY 24 / 9:15 PM

*I*WAS PAST that stage in my life. I shouldn't find him sexy. All those tattoos and that crazy messy hair. No. The last guy I'd dated that looked like him had ended up in jail. He'd thought running from the cops was a good idea instead of pulling over and taking the ticket. I'd had to call my brother to come get me after my ride had been arrested.

Walking directly to the bar, I poured myself a glass of single malt whiskey then headed for the stairs. As tempting as it was to watch the new Eli handle his angry family, I was afraid my attraction to him would just get worse. I'd been attracted to him enough back when he'd been the clean-cut, dependable sort. This, however, was way more intriguing. Which was typical of me. I made terrible choices when it came to men. Eli had let me see him. He's not flinched when our eyes were locked. I saw the difference there. He was not the same guy. I shivered slightly as I remembered the haunted look he'd not even tried to mask. Was it his gran's cancer causing such obvious pain? I couldn't wrap my head around it, but I didn't think that was it. There was a knowledge there. One that almost warned those that got close enough to keep their distance.

"It's about damn time." Bliss's father's voice made me pause and I closed my eyes tightly a moment. Battling over the option to stay and watch this or get away from it. The guy I'd just met outside wasn't who they all thought he was. The easy-going happy Eli was gone and I wanted to warn them all to be careful. Which seemed silly but at the same time I thought both Eli and the others needed a proper introduction. They didn't know this Eli at all, and I wondered if he remembered them. If he remembered how important they had always been to him. Because the guy outside didn't seem to give a shit that he was hurting them all by his absence.

"Good to see you too, Cage," Eli's drawl was deep, and I bit my bottom lip thinking that his darkness did things to me that I should be ashamed of. I needed to just keep walking up the steps and forget this night. Forget Eli and all his hidden issues and sexiness.

"Gran left an hour ago," a female voice added.

No response from Eli. I paused and waited for him to speak. When a few seconds went by with nothing I gave up on my good sense and I turned around on the stairs to see what was happening. Eli's sister Crimson was glaring at him with a hand on her hip. She was waiting for a response. It was a stand-off that she was going to lose because Eli cocked one eyebrow at her and waited. If she wanted a sibling quarrel, she wasn't going to get one with him.

Everyone in the room had remained silent. Like me, they were all watching the scene unfold. Possibly waiting on an explanation from Eli I knew they would never get. Their silence, his void almost bored expression confused them all and it was making me nervous for him or maybe I was nervous for them. Hell, I didn't know who to be worried about which was ridiculous.

"Don't let me interrupt," Eli said, lifting his gaze from his sister to give the rest of the room a glance. Then he walked past his sister toward the food still out on the table. Bliss moved quickly then and went to meet him. Everyone eased back into conversation but it was still much quieter than it had been, it seemed forced now. As if everyone was still focused on Eli. Trying to figure him out and confused by what they had just seen. I was right there with them. I may not have grown up knowing him my entire life, but I'd been around him enough to know this was all unexpected. But then so had his running off after the wedding. At first, I had assumed like everyone else it had been his way of dealing with Bliss getting married to my brother. And it still may possibly have been. Whatever the reason for his running off he wasn't returning the same guy. The one who had loved Bliss since he was a boy was gone. This was not about Bliss.

"Is no one gonna fucking mention all the damn ink and the hair?" The deep voice came from the corner of the living room. Jimmy Taylor was pointing at Eli with the whiskey glass in his hand and grinning as if he wanted to either toast Eli or laugh. I wasn't sure.

I held my breath. Jimmy Taylor was a cut up. Never serious. He was trying to lighten the mood, but I wasn't sure it was possible to ease Eli's mood.

I turned back to Eli, and I fought the urge to close my eyes. This may all go very bad very quickly.

"You want some of this. Don't act like you don't," Eli replied and although he didn't smile. Which was a shame because I knew Eli had a great smile, he did appear relaxed. Not confrontational.

Jimmy laughed then and the tension in the room eased. "Fuck

yeah I do. Good boy gone bad. Sexy as hell."

Eli gave a shrug of his shoulders. "I did it all for you," he told Jimmy and that got laughter from others in the room.

I let out a sigh of relief. Why I cared so much about how this all went down, I had no idea. This didn't affect me at all. These weren't my people. I barely knew them. Some more than others. I tried to remember most of their names, but that was hard. Then figuring out who went with who and was related to who . . . that was a clusterfuck and I needed a family tree to keep in my pocket as a cheat sheet.

One of Bliss's brothers stood up and I couldn't remember his name. They all looked alike and they all had names that started with C. It was equally confusing. "I think we should all just be thankful Saffron isn't here for this," he announced loudly. As if he were speaking to a crowd much larger than the people in the room.

"Amen!" one of the other guys around his age called out. Didn't know who he was, but he had blonde surfer looking hair.

"Don't y'all start in on Saffron when she's not here to defend herself," Bliss's mother, Eva, scolded. She was giving her son a warning look.

"They'd say the same shit if she was here. We all know she deserves it," Jimmy said with a shrug. I'd heard stories about Saffron from Bliss. I'd seen her once at the wedding and she was stunning, but she knew it. I'd seen her weld her beauty unfairly which I thought made her less attractive. The twin she had was her complete opposite. Which in my opinion made the twin the truly beautiful one.

The multiple conversations all began to start back up as if nothing had happened. I let my gaze go back to Eli who was talking to Nate. My brother didn't look pleased with Eli, but Bliss was there at Nate's right arm. She was saying something to my brother. Unlike the rest of the laughter and laid back conversations in the room, theirs seemed tense. Nate wouldn't care about the difference in Eli. His dark scowl and darker mood would only piss Nate off more. Because in Nate's eyes, Eli was upsetting Bliss and my brother didn't allow his wife to be upset. I'd seen my father react to situations involving my mother my entire life. The men in my family were ridiculously protective of their women. Eli didn't know this I was sure and I was tempted to go save him.

I didn't necessarily think he deserved it. Being late tonight was a douchebag move. But I wasn't so sure that he'd done it to be an ass. There was more to this change. It was possible he was dealing with his gran's diagnosis in his own way and he needed space to accept it. Whatever the reason, I didn't think my brother was considering any of this as he spoke to Eli.

Bliss was saying something to both of them and Eli looked as if he were somewhere else. Her words not even registering. The uninterested expression said more than he realized. Even though I knew good and well I should go upstairs and read a book . . . in a bubble bath . . . alone, minding my own business, I went back down the stairs I'd climbed.

I made my way back through the room and I was almost to the small group when Eli's eye caught my approach and he turned his attention fully on me. Had I ever realized how amazing his eyes were before tonight? No . . . I didn't think so. Until we had spoken outside, I had never truly looked at Eli closely. He'd just been Bliss's best friend. His eye never being something I wanted to explore. The way they locked on me now was a bit unsettling. If I was a weaker woman, I would have turned around and left for the bedroom. The secrets I wasn't sure I ever wanted to know locked inside those green pools were too damn intriguing to walk away from. It wasn't that he appeared happy to see me either. Heck, he didn't even look relieved.

The man could at least appreciate the fact I was here to save him from a situation he didn't want to be in. I could see that from across the room. It wasn't like I had come over here to flirt with him or get his attention. Even if he didn't disturb me slightly with his odd behavior, I wouldn't consider him relationship potential.

Eli Hardy was not an option. He was my sister-in-law's best friend or he had been. The new Eli I wasn't so sure felt the same. But he had been in love with her when she'd met Nate. He may not have loved Lila Kate when they had dated, but he'd been pretty damn attached to her when I first met him. Those two connections made him off limits. I didn't think there was a girl code for something that complicated, but I was sure it would be a big NOPE if it ever was dissected.

"Hey, y'all are monopolizing the most interesting person in the room," I said in a light teasing voice as I stepped up beside my brother and just inches away from Eli.

Nate shot me a glance as if to decide what I was up to. I could see his eyes studying me hard. I winked at him then turned my attention back to Eli. "They all got a look at you. Your parents have left with your gran. Want to walk me down the beach so I can get a break from all these voices?"

His eyes narrowed for a brief second. The flirting was a bit much for even me, but I was going with it for the sake of the audience in the room. Surely Eli could see that.

"Or you could stay in here and listen to my brother bitch, possibly get verbally scolded by your sister again." I pretended to glance around to see who else was here although I already knew. "There's also your aunt Larissa who I see coming this way. She's gonna hammer your ears too, I imagine."

Eli followed my gaze to see I wasn't lying about Larissa. She was headed this way.

"Fuck," he muttered.

"What did you expect?" Bliss whispered.

Eli turned his head and his eyes came back to me. Before he could say anything, Larissa was there. "When did you become a little shit? Hendrix has always reserved that role in the family." Larissa sounded more disappointed than anything. I had no idea who Hendrix was, but Eli didn't seem insulted.

"He's still a shit," Eli replied.

"Was it his comments this morning at breakfast that kept you from showing up like a decent human being tonight?" Larissa asked.

I was intrigued and maybe a little nosey. If Eli didn't look so uncomfortable, I'd let this go on so I could figure out who Hendrix was and what he'd said to Eli. Right now, I was on a rescue mission even if I didn't want to be.

"Eli, can you take me on that walk now?" I asked him and all four pairs of eyes swung to me. I ignored them all but Eli's of course. I smiled sweetly at him. "You did promise," I added.

Nate didn't like me getting involved. I could tell without looking at my brother. He could get over it.

"Yeah," Eli replied, and he nodded his head for me to start walking and he'd follow.

I managed a bright smile that was so fake it was ridiculous to the other three standing there then turned on my heels and made my way to the French doors overlooking the gulf. Before I reached the exit, Eli moved in front of me and opened a door then stood back so I could go outside. There was the guy I remembered. The gentleman everyone loved. But as quickly as he appeared with the opening of the door, it was gone. No smile. No thank you for the rescue. Not even silent eye contact.

I slid off my heels and left them at the top of the stairs then headed down toward the sand below barefoot. The breeze was warm, so my arms weren't chilled. Summer wasn't officially here until the solstice, but in South Alabama, it had most definitely arrived.

The moon was full and walking beside Eli in the silence felt nice. There was no need to talk if he didn't want to. We'd done that already. I hadn't gotten him out here to talk anyway. I was tired of talking today. I'd done more than I usually did. Besides, Eli had little to say. No need to force him to speak.

The house was just a light in the distance when he finally spoke.

"Why did you do that?" he asked.

I lifted a shoulder to give a half shrug. Still no thank you. Not even the sound of gratitude. "You looked like you needed an escape."

"I did," he agreed.

"I was headed upstairs to escape myself. But I couldn't ignore my hero mentality and let a poor guy get eaten alive by angry females."

"Hmmm," was his only response. What did that mean? And why did it have to sound so raspy and sexy? I should be annoyed by his lack of response. Not turned on by a deep husky rumble.

Back off Ophelia. Don't go there. You already discussed this with yourself. He is off limits. Girl code unscripted or some shit.

"I owe you one." His voice and words surprising me. That was as close to a thank you I was going to get, but I'd take it. Besides if he was gushing over me and appreciative would I be as attracted to him? I knew that answer and I was going to pretend I didn't. It made me sound shallow. I hated shallow. Needing to get out of my own head, I decided I'd do the small talk thing. Or attempt it with him.

"No, I think we are even now. I owed you one," I told him.

I felt his gaze on me then. Meeting that gaze was a stupid idea.

I did it anyway. Because tonight I was being all kinds of stupid. Even out here in the moonlight, those eyes of his were something.

"Why did you owe me?" he asked, and I was suddenly as mesmerized by his lips as I had been his eyes. What was I doing? Snap out of this, Ophelia! I jerked my gaze off him and looked straight ahead again.

"The wedding. You saved my sanity by sharing your whiskey. Got me through that day." I wasn't just saying that either. I was serious. I'd been stressed out until my little visit with Eli on the bench under the beautiful live oak tree. He'd made me smile, given me enough drink to calm my nerves, and I enjoyed his drunken company.

"That's all blurry. I'd had way too much of that whiskey. It was a good thing I shared some of it," he said.

"Do you remember our talk at all?" I asked, feeling a little deflated that it was blurry for him. Not that it mattered. It wasn't like I had dwelled on it over the past year. Just because he was here with me in the moonlight walking down the beach with his new brooding and mysterious sex appeal . . . no big deal.

I chanced a glance at him, and he was smirking. It wasn't a smile. The smirk didn't even crinkle his eyes. No real amusement in its appearance. More like he remembered it but it held no importance to him and he seemed to understand I wanted it to. If that even made sense.

"The way you smell. I remembered that. It's the same."

Not the response I was expecting. I needed him to elaborate on that. Did I smell bad? Did he like it? Did he think about it often? Come on Eli . . . I'm a female, I need more.

I waited. He said nothing.

"That's all. My smell," I coaxed finally.

When I thought he wasn't going to say more, he slowed to a

stop and looked up at the moon then toward me. I'd also stopped walking. "I believe I told you that you looked hot as fuck." He added that bit as if we were talking about the weather. He didn't turn to see my expression or flash me a teasing grin. He seemed to be thinking of something completely different than the conversation we were having. His profile was hard, masculine, and the lack of interest pouring off him sent out a challenge I didn't think he realized. Add that thick, deep voice and he most likely got girls naked within seconds. No, no, no . . . stop that. I was not going to think about sex with Eli. I WAS NOT. He certainly wasn't thinking about it with me. Where was my pride, for crying out loud? I was better than this.

"You did say that," I replied, finally remembering his drunken words and how at the time I thought he was sweet. A word so foreign to the man in front of me now. There was nothing sweet left in him.

"I was so fucking naïve," he said, more thoughtful now. His eyes held a seriousness in them. A knowledge of things the old Eli didn't possess. What had this Eli seen, done, experienced that changed him so much? His head turned toward me then. Our eyes meeting. It frightened me somewhat. I wasn't sure what he was looking for, but like earlier, it seemed like he was searching for more.

I stood there letting the waves crashing behind us be the only sound. Although the way he studied me so intently made me feel exposed. I also knew there was nothing I truly had to hide from him. Allowing him to search for whatever he seemed to want to find was hard, but I remained still. And I did some searching of my own.

It was me who broke eye contact first. My chest ached from something I couldn't explain and for a moment I missed the guy

I'd never gotten to know. He wasn't inside there anymore.

"It's probably safe to return," Eli said. "They've all got to leave eventually."

Then he started walking back.

I didn't follow right away. I watched him for a few moments while I mentally scolded myself for being affected by him so much. I had one objective and that had been to rescue him from his family. I'd done that. It was over. There was no reason to long for his company when he obviously wasn't desiring mine.

There was a good chance I wouldn't see Eli Hardy again for months or even years. Our paths had no real reason to cross. The thought wasn't the relief it was meant to be. Instead, I missed him already.

He stopped walking and glanced back at me. The darkness shadowed his face. I began to move in the direction he was toward the house. He waited until I caught up to him then fell into step beside me. No words. Nothing more.

It was as odd as he was but also comforting. I didn't feel like I had to say anything or that talk was expected of me. We just walked on in silence.

Chapter Six

~ELI HARDY~

MAY 25 / 10:23 AM

DISTANCE. I NEEDED some distance. From everyone's fear, concern, tears, all of it. This morning wasn't even over and yet it felt like days since we'd been in the waiting room. There were still hours left to go. At least that was what we had been told to expect.

Getting outside of the hospital and its smell that brought back all the times I'd basically lived in one while Bliss had been there. The smell triggered memories I didn't want to think about. The last time I'd stepped in a hospital had been the hardest moments a man could face. My soul had been ripped from me. I would never be the same. Yet, facing another kind of pain, I was back inside the walls of one while the sorrow from my past taunted me.

I stepped outside the sterile building into the fresh air, I felt instant relief. It would be brief, but it was needed. Reality was still the same. My gran was still in there and we would know today how long she had to live. That wasn't going away. But the mother-fucking smell that haunted me was gone for now. I could breathe.

"Donuts? A few even have bacon on them. I hear they're really good." The sound of Ophelia's voice managed to pull me from the heaviness with an instant calming effect. I soaked that in before turning to see her standing a few feet behind me with a large bag in her hand. "I would have brought coffee too. I'm sure the coffee in there is awful, but there's too many of y'all and only one of me."

I glanced at the bag in her hand before taking in her smile again. Wanting to look at her wasn't anything I should get attached to or even dwell on. Even knowing this, I enjoyed the view anyway. She was hard not to appreciate. Even if I didn't want to admit it, her presence soothed the reckless ache inside me.

"Donuts with bacon?" I asked her instead of telling her that just getting to look at her was sufficient. It was all I would ever allow myself to do and even that much was dangerous. There was nothing good that would come of that. Besides, Ophelia Finlay had her own walls. I'd seen them a year ago and they were still standing. Her eyes were expressive even when she was trying to hide her thoughts. I knew she had walls just like I knew she had seen the difference in me everyone else had been confused over. But she wasn't asking. She wasn't pressing me with questions. She was accepting there were reasons and letting me keep my secrets.

"I've not had them myself. I prefer chocolate glaze on my donuts, but this place is so popular if you don't get in line early you don't get the donuts. They sell out. I was in line at seven this morning and by the time I got up there, they only had three of the bacon ones left. So, if you want to try one, you need to grab it now. Before your family gets a hold of this bag," she said, holding the bag up for me to take.

It was a large paper bag with two sturdy handles. I quickly

took it because I was sure it was heavy. Not because I wanted the bacon donut. That didn't sound appealing even if I loved bacon. I appreciated Ophelia's kind gesture and I knew my family would too.

The bag was heavier than I thought. "How many donuts did you buy?" I asked.

She sighed with the weight of the bag gone. "You've got a large family," she stated the obvious. "A lot."

"This was nice of you. Getting in line at seven though was more generous than necessary." I wanted to keep her out here with me. I didn't want to go back inside. I'd keep her and the damn donuts out here with me in a bubble if I could.

"Today's a hard day. I know donuts don't make it easier, but I wanted to do something."

Her being here was enough. At least for me. The rest of them would appreciate the donuts for sure. They probably knew about the damn popular donuts. It was nice of her. I didn't need any other reason to like this woman.

"Are you okay?" she asked me then and the concern in her eyes shouldn't feel good. I was letting her get too close and I already knew the trouble that came with trusting or caring.

"I'm good. It's been a tough morning." I nodded my head toward the doors. "Aunt Amanda is having the hardest time with it all. Preston has had to hold her constantly. She's crying a lot." I was deflecting and oddly enough she realized it. The way her eyes slightly narrowed gave it away. She studied too closely. I had to be careful with that. She may not ask questions, but she didn't miss what was said in the silence.

"I can't imagine how she feels. If I was facing this with my mother, I'd be the same." She wasn't just saying that to make me feel better. The sincerity was as clear as her other reactions. There was no bullshit with Ophelia. The blunt honesty was so damn refreshing I was finding my need to keep her talking was growing.

"Dad hasn't broken down and I almost expected it when they took her back this morning. He's not talking though. He just sits and stares straight ahead. Mom has his hand in hers and she's beside him whispering things to him occasionally, but mostly they sit in silence. She got up once for coffee and Dad looked so damn lost without her it was too much to look at. I've never seen my dad scared before." I stopped talking. Shit was just pouring out of me that I hadn't even realized was bothering me. How was I suddenly needing to talk about it to a woman I barely knew?

"Is that why you're out here? To get away from it for a while?" she asked.

"Yeah." *No.* It hadn't been why, but now I realized possibly it was a part of the reason.

She reached for the bag in my hands. "Let me take this inside. You go find a quiet spot and recharge."

I didn't hand over the heavy bag. I held it unsure if I could go back in there just yet, or if I had to make myself so she would leave. Keeping her here was not something I should entertain. The more I opened up and relaxed with her the more difficult this would become.

"Will you come back?" I asked. My mouth completely ignoring my head. What the fuck was I doing?

"Do you want me to?" she asked, her eyes so damn sincere. She would return to me out here. All I had to do was say I wanted her to and she was back. This would not end well. I should thank her and take the huge bag inside. Forget the way she affected me. I should but today . . . I wasn't going to be able to.

"Yeah, I do." Fuck it, that was the truth. Today I could accept the fact I was weak. My emotions raw and her being here made that easier. For whatever reason it was. Possibly the voodoo I'd experienced last night.

She smiled then. As if my blunt honest answer was exactly what she wanted to hear. "I'll be right back. I promise," she said then took the bag and I watched as she entered the hospital.

When the automatic doors closed behind her, I scanned the area for somewhere to go. Standing at the entrance wasn't far enough away and anyone who came by to check on things would see me. I'd have to talk to them. They wouldn't be Ophelia and therefore I wouldn't be interested in speaking.

I wasn't going to think too hard about why I wanted Ophelia close. Just her company. I'd given up overthinking shit this past year. I just went with it. Lived life and knew regret would always be there. Just as I knew I wouldn't change the past even if I could. My actions would have still been the same outcome. Except I'd have seen my gran this past year. That I would change. I regretted missing out on Christmas at her house. What if it had been the last year she was alive for the holidays and I'd missed it? Even though I would want to go back and be here that would have been impossible too. Because the events that had happened during that time had brought me to my lowest point. I'd been unable to see anyone then. I didn't even remember Christmas Day. Darkness slowly came with the sorrow attached to those days. I'd worked hard to find my balance again.

I slammed a fist into the trunk of a tree three times until the skin broke on my knuckles and I saw the blood. Didn't fix shit and the small sting of pain wasn't enough. Regret wasn't something you could control. One small detail Grate O'Neill hadn't told me. But then Grate had lived a much different life than mine. Maybe regret wasn't an issue for him at all.

The day I'd walked into his shop to get my first tattoo I'd been so damn naïve he'd taken pity on me. Taught me things. Shown me a world I hadn't lived before. Without Grate, I wondered if I would have come through any of the things that followed. Grate hadn't been through the pain I had been trying to fight through, but his had been just as intense and it had been longer. He'd lived a life so very different than mine.

"You're bleeding." Ophelia's voice brought me back to the here and now. I glanced down at my hand before I looked at her. She was already taking a seat on the grass beside me. I felt bad about not sitting a few feet over on the wooden bench, but she seemed fine with joining me on the grass.

"Yeah, I had a moment," I said with no more explanation.

Ophelia opened her purse and pulled out a tissue then handed it to me. "Clean it up some with this," she said then continued to dig. I watched her as I absently wiped away the blood. The tissue wasn't going to do much, but I wasn't going to be rude and point it out.

Then she lifted a small pink animal print container from her purse and opened it. I watched as she began taking out first aid items.

"You carry around antiseptic wipes and bandages in your purse?" I asked amused.

She was busy opening one of the small square antiseptic wipes, but she lifted her gaze to me. "Are you mocking me?" she asked.

I shook my head, and in that moment, I felt like grinning. It was so fucking foreign to me now it startled me. I noticed she was fighting back her own smile. It was cute. Ophelia Finlay may look like an angel, but her reputation wasn't that spotless. She had a badass quality that made being near her easier. I knew my demons and although she didn't ever need to know them, I felt like she was tough enough to venture close and not get burned. The first aid kit in her purse did not fit how I thought of her.

"My mom still stuffs our stockings at Christmas," she said as she went back to work now cleaning my knuckles herself with the wipe. The alcohol burned like a son of a bitch, but I didn't flinch. "She gave all the girls one of these this year." Ophelia shrugged then opened a bandage. "I tossed it in my purse and so far this is the second time it's come in handy."

Not wanting her to stop talking I asked, "When was the other time?"

She finished with me then closed her little kit. "I cut my arm climbing over something."

The way her cheeks turned slightly pink made me even more curious. "What?"

She tossed the container back into the small white purse then put her hands in her lap and sat with her back straight before meeting my gaze. "A fence."

That one word made her cheeks even brighter. "Why were you climbing a fence?" I wasn't letting her out of this. I needed the story. From the way she was fidgeting with her hands, I knew it would take my mind off the shit in my head.

"Does that really matter?" she asked and gave me an innocent smile that did not belong on a Finlay's face. Not even this angelic looking one. But damn she looked good trying.

"Yeah, it does." The challenging tone in my voice had her narrowing her eyes. I waited while she debated telling me or continuing to stall. Either way, I had her attention and I was good with it. She made the other stuff fade away and I needed that more than anything else.

She shifted on the ground, but that regal poise of hers didn't relax. How she could make sitting there without a slight slouch in her shoulders look so damn natural was beyond me. It was a talent I'd never actually seen before. The long pale hair of hers, that I knew from seeing her mother's hair wasn't from a bottle, draped over her left shoulder. She cocked her head slightly to the left and I watched as it brushed the cleavage she was showing with the low-cut Guns and Roses vintage tee shirt she was wearing. It had been altered at some point by being cut in a V-shape at the neck and cropped to just hit her waist. Most people would assume it was bought this way and not an original. But her grandfather was a rock legend and I knew the shirt was, in fact, a legit Appetite for Destruction 1987 tour shirt. That kind of vintage you couldn't manufacture.

"Fine," she sighed dramatically. "I was climbing the fence of a guy's house that I had been dating." When she paused this time, a slow wicked grin touched her lips. It didn't matter what she said as long as she kept smiling like that. Damn if it wasn't a welcome distraction. "He had wanted us to be exclusive and I'd decided I didn't want to see him anymore. It got ugly at least on his part so I left in a hurry. But when I got home, I went to take off my jewelry and remembered my grandmother's bracelet was still on the table beside his hot tub. In my need to get the hell away from there, I'd forgotten the bracelet. My mother's mother passed away before I was ever born. My grandfather had the bracelet and gave it to my mother the day I was born as a gift. The day I graduated high school my mother gave it to me. It's a very special bracelet." She focused on something over my shoulder and for a moment her thoughts had gone somewhere else. Why was I so interested in her, in what she was thinking, in every damn thing about her?

"I wasn't sure if he'd give it back or just continue to be dramatic. I didn't want to see him again and hoped to avoid him until he got over us. So, I just waited until the middle of the night when I knew he'd be asleep and went back to get it."

There was the urge to smile tugging at me, but I couldn't. Not even with the image of Ophelia climbing a fence. Allowing myself to smile felt like a betrayal that I couldn't face right now. I used the humor to distract me enough to push back the darkness that followed these thoughts. Yet the image of Ophelia scaling a fence to go retrieve her bracelet just because she wanted to avoid a man had been enough to make me want to smile. She made me forget the bad. Nothing I'd tried, no female, no activity, nothing had been able to make me want to move on in life the way she did. The way Ophelia saw life, went after it, lived it, made me want to be close to her. As terrible of an idea as that was. Why did it have to be this woman that brought back the life in me I didn't think existed?

She had no idea the inner battle inside me. That her presence was causing more conflict than I wanted to deal with. To her I was a guy, dealing with the news my grandmother could very well leave this world soon. She thought she was distracting me or entertaining me. The beauty beside me had no idea she was breathing life where I thought there wasn't any.

"I was unaware you were a criminal." I finally said something. I knew she had hoped for more from me. A smile or a laugh. She'd gone out of her way to be dramatic with her storytelling. If she only knew how close to smiling without realizing it I'd been. The power she had to give me a rare moment of amusement.

She rolled her eyes. "I'm not a criminal. I was taking back what was mine." She was fighting back a smile now. "Besides, I didn't get caught."

"But you have been arrested," I reminded her. I'd heard Bliss mention it before.

She pretended to look annoyed but the pride in her blue eyes were unmistakable. "It was a misunderstanding."

I was sure it was. Little rebel. I didn't push for more.

"It's a good story," I told her instead.

"I got the bracelet back. That's the important part." She paused and then added, "I also passed the cops as they sped by me on the way to his house. I didn't know his security system triggered when one entered the backyard."

The instant tug on the corners of my lips might have won that time before I could do anything to stop it. Instead of feeling instant guilt, it was pleasant.

Chapter Seven

♥ OPHELIA FINLAY ♥

MAY 26 / 2:43 PM

I LOOKED FORWARD to Sundays in the summer. They normally included sleeping late, eating brunch at the Kerrington Club with my parents, then enjoying a book while sitting under an umbrella on the sand. The smell of the salty breeze and the pina colada in my hand, mixed with the sound of the waves. It was perfect solitude.

Today, however, I was battling some unknown funk that I'd been in since arriving home just before noon. I'd woken up to the smell of breakfast. Bliss had grown up on a farm and she made the best biscuits and gravy I'd ever eaten. She also believed in bacon, sausage cheese grits, and eggs to go with the biscuits and gravy. It was a miracle my brother wasn't fat with the way she cooked. But then neither were her brothers or her father.

I had enjoyed my morning talking with my brother and sister-in-law before packing up the few things I had in the bathroom and heading home. They were happy and I wanted that for Nate. He'd been in a toxic relationship when he'd met Bliss. One I had tried to warn him about. He had thought it was what he wanted but seeing Bliss again had shown him what real love was. She made him smile and that was enough for me. I didn't worry about my brother anymore. Now I could focus all my worry on my sister. I wasn't going to think about Phoenix right now though. I'd do that later. Besides, Phoenix wasn't answering my calls and according to Nate, she was ignoring his too. We had discussed her for awhile this morning. I was home and needed to focus on me. Or whatever was bothering me.

Typically, the sight of home made me feel content.

Today though nothing was the same. I was in a terrible mood and putting on my bikini, grabbing a book, then heading across the street to find a spot on the sand didn't sound at all appealing. Instead, I was sitting on the sofa in my sweats watching *Game of Thrones* from the beginning again and eating leftover Easter candy. I didn't want to think about what had caused this funky mood. I would then have to accept it and dissect it. Neither things I was willing to do. Instead, I'd watch Jason Momoa have a lot of sex and I'd eat chocolate. Seemed rational.

The ringing of my phone interrupted my thoughts and I paused the episode although I'd already seen this season twice. I happened to enjoy an almost naked Momoa as did the rest of the females on planet earth. Like I always did, I would tell Daenerys Targaryen that her tears were ridiculous when that man was the one screwing you. Sure, she couldn't hear me and talking to the television was weird, but I did it anyway.

I grabbed my phone just as the Khal Drogo took his wife from behind and smiled at the fact it was paused on that image. An unknown number lit my screen. Sea Breeze, Alabama was all it told me. Staring at the sex scene frozen on my screen I decided I'd answer the phone. Although I typically sent all un-known calls. . . . And some callers I did know to voicemail. My voicemail would then tell them that texting me was best. I didn't listen to voicemail. Today though was the caller's lucky day be-cause it said Sea Breeze.

"Hello," I said quickly.

"You left." The deep voice that came over the line made me feel warm. Deep down I'd wanted it to be him. I had just been too cautious to let myself admit it.

"Eli," I said, realizing that I was smiling as I said his name.

There was a pause and I had a moment where I wondered if I had been wrong about the voice on the other line. Had I wanted it to be Eli so badly I had thought this was him?

"I went to see if you wanted to get lunch and Bliss said you'd left this morning." It was Eli. Relief and excitement returned. It had been a long time since a man made me feel so giddy. My emotions were all over the place with this guy. Normally I ran from this or the idea of this but I craved everything to do with him. Yesterday I'd wanted to climb in his lap and kiss him until I was satisfied. I knew that was the wrong reaction to a guy who was outside a hospital dealing with grief over his gran's illness. But my hormones had not seemed to care. They were lusting while he suffered.

The fact he had come to see me today made everything seem brighter. My chest was light and the melancholy mood gone. I didn't even care that it was a guy making me feel this way. Al-though I knew that most men caused problems and when they had this kind of power over your emotions, they could break you, I embraced it anyway.

"I have work tomorrow," I told him. We had sat outside yes-terday for three hours talking. Until his mom had texted him that his grandmother was out of surgery and he was needed. I hadn't gone inside with him. It wasn't my place, but I hadn't wanted to leave him either. My mood had gone south the moment I watched him walk inside the hospital.

Bliss had told me that evening that they'd found the cancer had spread and chemotherapy could give her time, but they weren't even promising a year. I'd gone to bed with an ache in my chest for everyone in their family but the sorrow I felt for Eli had been deep. I knew words of comfort were just that . . . words. It didn't help. Getting Eli's number from Bliss so I could call him was pointless. He needed his family, not some woman he barely knew calling to tell him she was what . . . sorry . . . praying . . . Hell, I didn't even pray. He had been dealing with inner turmoil yesterday and I'd been trying to make him smile and imagining crawling all over him. Women with that kind of selfish mindset didn't pray. God wouldn't listen to us anyway. He knew we were full of bullshit.

"I know. I just hoped I'd see you one more time before you had to go," he replied. My chest did that fluttery thing that I'd experienced last when I'd had a crush on a guy in eleventh grade and he smiled at me. I was being that silly over Eli Hardy. I needed to be slapped.

I should mention his grandmother at this moment. Say something to him, condolences maybe . . . but I wasn't good at this kind of thing. I never had understood why people said things at times like this that didn't help. If they could do something, then do it. That I understood. It's why I took the donuts to the hospital. That was an action, not a promise for "prayers" or "keeping you in my thoughts" because honestly who cared about being in someone's thoughts. They didn't need my prayers and what good were my thoughts to them. I decided to forgo mentioning it at all. I was sure he'd heard enough from everyone else.

"If I had known you wanted to have lunch I'd have stayed," I decided honesty was also something I could do here. Might as well not be vague with a man who just found out his grandmother was going to die. He had called me, gone by to see me.

"I should have come over sooner," he said then, and I heard the regret in his tone.

"You have a lot going on right now. Letting some female know you want to have lunch probably isn't the first thing on your mind and I don't blame you." Which was also true. I added then because I had to say something. Even if words could give no comfort here. "I'm sorry, Eli." That again was the truth. My telling him didn't help, but I was sad for him and the rest of his family.

"What about dinner?" he asked then instead of replying to my "I'm sorry."

I'd been ready for an awkward response, not a question about my next meal. That confused me. "Dinner?" I asked, thinking I could have possibly misunderstood him.

"If I get on my bike now, I'll be there in time for dinner."

He was asking me if he could drive all the way here just to take me to dinner. "If you're willing to drive that far for dinner then the least I could do would be to cook for you." I was not the best cook. What the hell was I saying? I had very few items in my wheelhouse that I could make successfully and none of them were real impressive.

"Leaving now. I'll see you before or at six."

"Okay." The simple word was not enough, but it's what I blurted out. I should say "Wait, I can't cook that well. Maybe we should get good food." Or "How about another time you need to be with family." Or anything other than . . ."Okay." But I didn't say more, and he didn't give me time to think it through further. The call ended and I stared down at my phone confused, surprised and obviously, I was excited. Before putting the phone down, I saved his number and then added a little smiley face emoji beside it with heart eyes. It may be ridiculous, but when I glanced at it from a distance, I would recognize the emoji even if it was too far to read his name.

With a quick glance around, I knew I had a lot to get done in a short time. I grabbed the chocolate and went to stick it back in the cabinet where it belonged. Then took the remote and pointed it at the television. "Sorry Khal Drago. I no longer need to watch you have sex to make me feel better." Which was saying a lot. Eli Hardy was more exciting than a naked Jason Momoa. I clicked off the television and laughed at my own habit of talking to the characters as if they could hear me. I would blame that on my living alone for so long, but the truth was I hadn't actually lived alone that long. Lila Kate had heard me talk to the television more than once when we lived together. It had been a topic of discussion often.

I quickly looked in my kitchen at the supplies I had to determine what I needed to go buy in order to cook an actual meal. Going to the grocery store wasn't something I enjoyed, but I found I was humming happily while I made a list and pranced . . . yes, I was prancing around my kitchen as well. When I caught a glimpse of my reflection in the window and saw the obvious joy, I paused.

My smile faded. My sour mood from earlier was gone. So quickly. The reason for my bad mood had been clear all along. I had noticed it and accepted it. But I hadn't thought about the future complications. I was the queen of emotional walls. I didn't let men get too close. Once I'd been young and loved freely. I had been taught the hard way that was stupid and painful. I walked into relationships with men carefully now. I didn't fully commit. I never trusted. I protected myself. Which men always got tired of this and either demanded something more and I ended things, or they gave up and walked away.

It had worked. I hadn't been hurt in a very long time. But when was the last time I was happy? When was the last time I felt this rush I was experiencing when I was near Eli? I couldn't remember. I'd forgotten how it could be.

Leaving Sea Breeze had meant leaving Eli Hardy. Even if I hadn't wanted to admit it that had bothered me. Now he was coming here, and I was happy again. The circumstances weren't great ones. Other than the fact he had only returned for his grandmother. There were other things like . . . the Eli Hardy that was safe no longer existed. The one you could depend on, the rule follower, the . . . good guy, was gone.

The Eli Hardy that existed now wasn't a guy anyone needed to get too attached to because he would leave again. That was the crux of it all. I was attracted to the one I could never trust with more than a good time. The guy he'd been before I'd never gotten to know. I never gave him a chance.

I shook my head and glared at myself in the window's reflection.

"Don't go making this into something it's not. He makes you smile. He's sexy and smart. Enjoy him while you can. Stop overthinking."

I wasn't sure if my reflection listened, but I felt better about it all.

Chapter Eight

~ELI HARDY~

MAY 26 / 5:39 PM

*T*HE LAST TIME I'd visited this apartment I'd been here for another woman. It was ironic that I was back. A place I never expected to return to. Not that I had any emotional damage from the time I'd spent with Lila. I knew now what I'd felt for her wasn't deep or real. Losing her to another man hadn't broken me. It hadn't done more than hit my ego. The woman that lived here now eased the real sorrow I held inside. That's why I was here. Ophelia did more to make me forget than the whiskey did.

The door opened before I reached it and Ophelia appeared. She was wearing a hot pink sundress that hung loosely and hit mid-thigh. She hadn't put on makeup and I liked it. The whole natural sexy look. Even her feet were bare. There was no attempt at trying to impress me.

"You made good time on that thing," she said. She was looking past me to my Harley.

"That thing goes as fast as a car does," I pointed out the obvious.

She lifted her left shoulder as if that meant nothing. "Dinner will be done in about fifteen minutes. But I have cream cheese stuffed jalapeños wrapped in bacon for an appetizer."

I hadn't eaten since this morning and the mention of food sounded good. "Thanks, I'm starving."

She beamed at that and I walked past her inside the studio to find it completely finished and very impressive. The last time I'd been here, it looked very different. Lila had done a lot with the place. "This turned out nice," I said as I scanned the area.

"Yeah, it's a great studio," Ophelia replied. "Lila Kate has put a lot of hard work into it."

I followed Ophelia to the back door. I knew the stairs that led to the flat were back there. Even if the place was finished now. It was the same layout structurally.

Watching Ophelia's perfectly rounded backside as she climbed the stairs was a bonus. I needed a distraction today and this was the best idea I'd had. When I had tried to think of what to do or where to go to get my mind off Gran . . . Ophelia had been the only thought in my head. She eased the inner turmoil like nothing else. Finding out that Gran's life was going to be cut short meant I wasn't leaving Sea Breeze as soon as I'd planned. I could go nowhere knowing my time with her was limited.

I needed a diversion from the thoughts roaring through my head. Ophelia was the perfect solution. Not only did she do an excellent job easing all the chaos inside me but she was safe because she didn't get attached to men. She was a free spirit with fucking walls protecting her from anything real. I'd laid in bed last night thinking about that and why she had those walls. There had to have been pain in her past that taught her to be careful. Protect herself. I knew neither of us were in danger of falling in love or wanting more. Which was why coming here was so easy. No one needed to love me. To love me would be tragic. For any woman.

The door swung open and Ophelia waved me inside. I noticed the difference immediately. The exposed beams and stainless steel appliances and countertops were the same. The industrial feel, however, wasn't as noticeable with the way it was now decorated. It was full of energy where once it had been more classically decorated. A mix match of color and a free wild style was the only way to describe it now. The furniture was eclectic. A bright blue sofa with pillows covered in yellow feathers on each end was the first thing that caught the eye when you entered the open flat. The massive painting of what was an abstract of what I recognized immediately as New Orleans French Quarter.

"Where did you get that painting?" I asked, nodding my head in the direction of it.

"It's amazing isn't it?" she said with a wistful smile. "It's Lila Kate's. I don't get to keep it. She's moving it to her master bedroom in her new house once she decides on the new furniture she wants in there. I can't remember who the artist is that painted it. I just know it's all the places that mean something to her and Cruz. Their story . . . I guess . . ." She trailed off then and looked away as if she realized I had been a part of that story too. It was her time in New Orleans with Cruz that she'd fallen in love with the bad boy and realized I wasn't what she wanted.

"He had it made for her then?" I asked, truly not at all bothered by the idea. I was glad Cruz Kerrington had turned it around before he lost the best thing that ever happened to him. I was also glad I hadn't loved a woman that could never love me equally. To Lila, I would have always been second best.

"Yes," Ophelia said then walked over to the kitchen. A bright blue toaster oven, espresso machine, and blender sat on the counters. The same blue was also the color of the hand towel and ceramic containers. I liked the way the place fit Ophelia's personality. She had made it hers.

She stirred the blue pot on the stove then went to check the oven. "Not too much longer," she said with a nervous smile. I was trying to figure out what had suddenly made her tense. "Here's a plate." She offered a small bright yellow plate to me that had the word EAT written on it in a bold blue print. "Help yourself to the stuffed jalapeños. I'll get you a drink."

I crossed the living area and took the plate from her by reaching over the bar. The stools were metal but painted bright colors with different faces that resembled works by Picasso on the backs of them.

"Do you want whiskey? Or red wine? I'm afraid I don't have beer."

I studied her a moment before speaking. "You went from relaxed to tense. Why?" I asked her bluntly. No point acting like her mood hadn't changed drastically within seconds.

Although she didn't respond right away, her eyes flicked very briefly over my shoulder toward the painting before she went to grab a glass from the cabinet. "I didn't realize I was tense," she replied. Like hell, she didn't.

I understood the difference in her demeanor now though. I'd missed it because she was so wrong with her train of thought that it hadn't dawned on me. Ophelia obviously believed I'd cared more for Lila than I had. "The painting," I began. "Lila and Cruz, our past, none of that bothers me. I was over it all before I drove out of Sea Breeze on Cruz's bike." No reason for her to think my baggage had anything to do with her boss and former roommate.

Her shoulders relaxed. It was very subtle, but I still noticed.

"She was never meant to be mine. I don't entertain the idea of anyone being my future. That belief is naïve."

Ophelia's smile fell some then. I couldn't think of why she wouldn't just agree. It was clear she felt the same way. She didn't open herself up to men the way most women did. My being honest about how I felt shouldn't put a damper on things for her. It should be a relief.

I took one of the jalapenos. "Whiskey will be fine," I answered her earlier question. Then I took a bite from the stuffed pepper in my hand and watched her begin fixing my drink.

"Ice?" she asked.

"Three cubes," I replied.

She cut her eyes at me with an amused expression and counted out three ice cubes before free pouring the whiskey. That was more than two ounces but not too much. She had a good eye.

When she placed the glass on the countertop in front of me, I finished off the appetizer in my hand. "These are amazing. Thanks for cooking. I'd have gladly taken you somewhere tonight. I didn't expect you to go to all this trouble."

"Don't thank me yet. Those stuffed jalapeños were a cheat. I bought them prepared at the deli across the parking lot. All I had to do was put them in the oven. This"—she waved to the other items cooking—"is one of the few things I can cook. It's nothing special and you may hate it. If you do, then you don't have to eat it."

I liked her honesty and ability to make fun of herself. She didn't care about impressing me or anyone for that matter. She didn't make excuses for things or try to be someone she wasn't. She was confident in who she was and didn't try to meet some higher standard to impress. That kind of self-worth was admirable. It was also sexy as hell.

"If it sucks, we can order pizza," I stated the obvious. Although I'd told her that I was good with taking her out, now I had her all to myself I didn't want to give that up.

"Mexican. If it sucks, we can order Mexican. There's a new

place in town and it's yummy. Besides, I have my heart set on tacos."

I almost said we could have gone there, but I didn't. If she wasn't going to lie about dumb shit neither was I. No reason to say I wanted to go out when I wanted to stay in. I came here to be near her and enjoy the way she made me feel. Staying away from everyone else would only make that calming effect her presence had on me stronger. I took another pepper and ate it while she pulled out what looked like tacos standing up inside some kind of slots that held them.

"It at least looks edible," she said with relief in her voice.

"If that's tacos, I've got to know what's in the pot. You stirred it a lot and I'm trying to figure out what could possibly go with tacos that needs to be cooking in a pot and stirred so often." My first thought had been beans or rice, but she'd worked over what was in the pot too much for it to be either.

"Queso," she replied with a wide grin. "I might not cook much, but I make killer queso. And they're not just any tacos. They're baked grouper tacos."

Right now, I would eat anything she put in front of me if I could just stay near her longer. This was the most peace I'd experienced in what felt like a lifetime.

Chapter Nine

♥ OPHELIA FINLAY ♥

MAY 26 / 7:40 PM

*I*KNEW AFTER the third glass of red wine I was at my limit. The fourth glass had been a dumb decision, but he had been smiling at my animated description of those who believe the earth is flat and it was such a rare thing for this new darker Eli to smile that I felt like I'd conquered the beast every time his lips curled up. It was as if I craved the sight. I was tipsy, but I was positive that if I was completely sober, I'd feel the same way.

Eli's hand was resting on my upper arm as I reclined back on his chest. We had taken our drinks to the sofa after dinner and continued our conversation about the belief in flat earth and how ludicrous it seemed. Then it had turned into a debate over man walking on the moon and had it actually happened. At some point between his fourth glass of whiskey and my third glass of wine we had turned on the television and where I had left *Game of Thrones* paused appeared on the screen.

Eli had given me a look as if he'd caught me being naughty before pressing play. I'd had to explain several things to him, but he seemed to be caught up and understanding what was happening. He had stretched out his arm and told me to lay back. I'd done so without question. This was how we'd finished two episodes and the rest of our drinks.

My focus had not been on the show but rather on how good he smelled. How hard his body was and how close his hand rested to my right breast. Lust had reared its head and I knew my breathing was a little quick. Although I was trying to control it and not get too carried away with my imagination. I knew I should call it a night, offer him the guest bedroom since he'd drank too much to drive and it was late, and then get up before I did something stupid. The wine had made this worse and I knew it.

The next episode was about to begin when Eli shifted away from me and I watched him set his glass down. Just the slight distance and space between us disappointed me. I'd been trying to get up, but the actual moving away from him hadn't been something I was prepared for. Before I could accept that our night was over and this delicious warmth I'd been in the past hour and a half had come to an end he leaned back and resumed his position.

Needy me snuggled right back against him like a damn puppy dog. I should be disgusted with myself, but this felt too good to care. I inhaled deeply and the scent of him made my nipples harden. I was getting lost in my own little sexual fantasy. The wine was to thank for this. Not that it took wine to make me want Eli Hardy. I wanted him without the wine. But the wine had made me clingy and unable to act like I wasn't wanting to crawl all over him.

"Ophelia." His voice was deeper and huskier than normal. I shivered a little and squeezed my thighs together. "You keep that up and I'm going to fuck you on this couch."

I froze. Just for a second. The word "fuck" had startled me as much as it had excited me. No man had ever warned me he was about to fuck me. A normal girl should be offended by that, right? Who wanted to be told they were going to get fucked?

Me.

Apparently, I wanted to be told by Eli Hardy that he was going to fuck me. Because I literally moaned with anticipation and grabbed his shirt in my fist as if I was making sure he didn't leave and that he followed through with his threat.

He turned his body slowly then moved over me until I was lying flat on my back and he was staring down at me. "Is that what you want?" His voice was hard and demanding. It only made me more crazed. "You want me to fuck you?"

"Yes," I whispered my eyes locked on his.

"Say it. Say you want me to fuck you." He ran a hand up my thigh and continued underneath the sundress I was wearing.

"I want you to fuck me," I said the words he wanted and grinned up at him wickedly. He wanted me to ask for it then I'd play that game.

He growled and the slow ease with which he had been moving changed. The sundress was jerked up and I lifted my upper body so he could remove it from me completely. I was left in nothing but the white lace panties I had chosen not thinking he'd see them but because they made me feel pretty. He stilled and his eyes took in my breasts and stomach before moving down to the panties. Both his hands reached for the sides of the lace and I lifted my hips so he could slide them down my legs. He did so quickly, not giving me time to adjust to my sudden nakedness.

I was bare. Nothing hidden from his eyes. I flushed, but the heat in his hungry glare was the cause, not embarrassment. He wanted this as much as I did. The ache between my legs grew stronger and I wiggled beneath him in a silent plea. He lowered his head in response and licked my left nipple before pulling it into his mouth and sucking hard. My cry of pleasure caused him to bite down as he moved his hand to slip it between my legs and run a finger deliberately over my sensitive clit. The sharp pain from the bite mixed with the satisfaction of his desired touch gave me an exquisite jolt.

"AH," I exhaled with a loud cry. His mouth moved to my right breast to suck, but his hand remained teasing me with rough large fingers. Sliding over the heat there and making me more crazed with desire than I'd ever been.

"This," he said, shoving a finger hard inside me as he held my gaze. "You want me inside here?" he was asking again. I was quivering beneath him like a maniac in need. What more did he require as affirmation I wanted him to fuck me. Just like he asked me already. I was willing and begging. If he didn't soon, I may die.

"Yes!" I sounded as desperate as I felt.

"Birth control?" he asked as he unzipped his jeans, keeping his eyes on me.

I nodded my head. Although no man had ever entered me without a condom on. I was very strict about safety. I should tell him. I should require he use one . . . but I realized in that moment no matter how bad Eli Hardy had gone, I trusted him. With this, I trusted him.

He grabbed my left leg and pulled it up higher in the crook of his arm. Our eyes held as he rocked his hips and filled me with one firm thrust.

The stretch of his entry made me go from sounds of gratitude to begging for it. He was thick and it stretched me. The pain from his size, however, was thrilling more than anything else. I'd never had a man in me with a cock this large. There was something to be said for it and I might become addicted. Each thrust touched the right spot without me having to maneuver my body to help him. How amazing was that? I became lost in the sensation not sure I'd survive this. How much pleasure could one person experience before it was too much?

"Holy fuck you're tight," he groaned, looking down at me. His pupils were large and the darkness in his eyes looked almost sinister. It was titillating. That ominous gleam staring down at me. His body covering mine. "So goddamn wet," he cursed but there was satisfaction in his tone.

His crude descriptions of my sex sent me straight into my first orgasm. I arched my back underneath him and clawed at his arms as it burst from deep inside me. I'd never orgasmed like this. Before this moment, all my orgasms had been from direct contact with my clit. This one was not, and I felt more moisture lubricate our joining. Had I done that? My body shook from the experience. I was unable to give it more thought. His breath was warm against my ear. I felt his lips brush just against my temple. My eyes wouldn't open yet and the heat from his breath against my neck caused me to shiver.

"That's just the first one, baby. I'm not about finished with this sweet pussy. Feels too damn good. Not sure I can stop fucking it." His words did exactly what he had known they would.

It ignited the fire inside me again. How many times would he be able to do this? As I panted and grabbed at his biceps, he pumped harder into me. I could see the same insane desperation in his eyes that I felt, and I lifted my hips to meet his thrust. Hungry to be there again. I began to scream his name as I burst into beautiful chaos deep inside and rode the waves of delight unaware of anything but how mind-blowing this was.

I was weak as I descended back to earth but when Eli pulled out of me, my eyes snapped open and I wanted to protest. Before I could form words to tell him I wanted more, he was lifting me up and turning me to lean me over the back of the sofa. My stomach pressed against the cushions and his hands grabbed my thighs and moved my legs farther apart. I understood then what he was doing, and I leaned forward more and jutted my bottom out toward him.

His large hands grabbed my waist in a tight grip, and he moved in from behind me. With one hard jerk, he pulled me back as he slammed into me. Stretching me again with his hard length. Making me moan loudly with my greed for more of what he could give me. He grabbed the back of my hair with one hand and squeezed my hip with the other. The control of the way he handled me should be frightening. But it wasn't. Eli was different. He wasn't the same guy I'd once met, but I trusted him without question.

"You asked me to fuck you," he said with a harsh tone that made me tremble. I liked it when he talked that way while he was inside me. "Now I don't think I can stop," he warned as he began to move faster with such hard thrusts the slapping of our bodies as he pumped inside me grew louder. As did his groans. "Yeah, fuck yeah, God your ass is perfect." He cupped both of my butt cheeks in his hands. "FUCK!" he shouted as the warmth from his release shot inside me. The heat, the way his body shook, the growing wetness now coating us both sent me into the third and final orgasm. Before the darkness wrapped me up and pulled me under. The freedom of letting it take me was beautiful.

Chapter Ten

~ELI HARDY~

MAY 27 / 5:03 AM

I'D BEEN DRESSED for well over thirty minutes. I should have left already. It was the right thing to do for both of us. Ophelia was without a doubt the best sex I'd ever had in my life. There wasn't even a close second. Being near her eased me and gave me peace that had become so foreign to me. She was like crisp spring water to a thirsty man.

I hadn't been prepared for how being inside her would affect me. That I didn't see coming. Until last night nothing had made me forget, feel like I had hope, gave me joy anymore. Not one damn thing I'd tried had relieved the despair so twisted inside me that I couldn't break free of it. Nothing that is until I'd been inside Ophelia. Sex wasn't meant to heal or move you. It was for pleasure. Last night had been pure lust. For both of us. We'd wanted each other and acted on it.

Finding myself again, the man I'd thought was gone, while

I fucked Ophelia was so damn tragic I didn't know how to wrap my head around it. Why couldn't I feel that way without sex being involved . . . hell without a woman being involved. I didn't want to connect with a woman again. I'd tried that, allowed myself to accept it, then I'd been marked for life because of it. Ophelia came into my life too late. Last night didn't change the events that had transpired the past year for me. If it could, I wouldn't be standing here trying to leave. I'd be in that bed still holding her.

What did that say about me? How fucked up was I that something as basic as hot sex could make me forget what I'd lost. What had been taken from me so unjustly. Was my soul as black now as I'd once accused . . . ? I closed my eyes before finishing that thought. I wouldn't think about her. Not here in this room with Ophelia lying there asleep. There was something pure about Ophelia and I knew it was part of my attraction. She deserved more than me. More than the way I'd spoken to her while I couldn't get enough of her last night. There had been no sweet words come out of my mouth and a woman like her deserved that. Not what I had given her. She was better than that. Yet another thing I had to be ashamed of in the predawn.

My leaving was in her best interest. I knew now that this connection with her was deeper for me than was good for her. If I'd only known this with her before I'd left, then things would have been so very different. I would have never ridden out of Sea Breeze. I would have never met . . . Alice.

"Are you going to stand there and stare at me until I wake up or leave without a goodbye?" Her voice was raspy from sleep and her eyes were still closed. I'd been too close to falling into the deep pit of agony thinking of my past to notice the change in her breathing and realize she was awake. I should have left sooner. Now I had to face this. Find a way to make it right and walk away.

"I wasn't sure. I was still debating." That was only partially true. I hadn't been debating. I knew I was going to leave. I had to leave. But the honesty wouldn't come. Nor would my resolve to leave her. "What's your preference?" I asked instead of making the decision myself.

She stretched and the blankets eased down just enough that it gave me a clear view of the tops of her breast. Remembering how they felt didn't help matters. I looked away from her and focused my gaze toward the window.

"I need coffee," she said instead of answering. "Go turn on the espresso machine and wait for me."

I simply nodded, knowing I should leave and knowing I wouldn't. Not until she was ready. I owed her more than a quick exit. The ease in which she was handling this also made it harder to go. Ophelia wouldn't be dramatic. I knew that, but deep down I wanted her to be more affected by the idea of me leaving. Accepting that weakness as one of many I had when it came to her was another reality.

Walking away from the view of her in the bed was a relief and disappointment. I'd never know what it was like to have her in that bed. To wake up with her curled up to me smiling from a night of wild sex. Fuck, the sorrow that came with knowing this was over before it began hit me harder than I expected. I didn't torture myself with looking over at the sofa. The images from last night would forever be burned in my brain. I didn't need any extra encouragement to dwell on it.

The kitchen was dark still before sunrise. I found the light switch and then went over to press the power button on the espresso machine. It was easy enough to find. After turning it on, I leaned back against the counter with my arms crossed over my chest and I waited patiently. Or appeared to be relaxed. I was wound tightly, and it wasn't going to ease as long as I was near her. Not after last night.

I knew she was thinking we would both feel better about this if we talked before I left. I owed it to her to let her believe she was right. I'd fucked her like a crazed man, talked to her harshly while doing it, and then shot my load into her without permission. I definitely owed her the talking she was wanting. Even if leaving would have been easier. I already knew the sex we had enjoyed wasn't going to change anything. We were consenting adults. She could reassure herself all of this. I'd give her that. She didn't need to know she'd fucked with my head. Made me want in a way I didn't think I could want anymore.

Her exit from the bedroom into the living area stopped all other thought. She hadn't bothered with brushing her hair. The thick blonde locks were in a disarray that reminded me of sex. She was wearing a large sweatshirt and a pair of men's boxers when she walked into the room barefoot. The bright pink on her toenails even managed to fascinate me. Damn, I needed to get some space between me and this woman.

She said nothing as she walked by me to begin making her coffee. I waited and when she said nothing, I started thinking maybe she expected me to speak first. The unwelcoming scowl on her face kept me from testing that theory. Instead I gave her time to get her coffee made and hopefully she'd speak soon.

Even if it was "get the fuck out of here." Which I would deserve and I'd also do without argument.

When she was finally done with the complicated coffee process, she held the cup in her hands and leaned back on the bar to face me.

"I may have drunk too much last night and gotten a little carried away. I remember it clearly though and I'm glad I did . . . we did." She laughed softly as if her stumbling over the words was funny. "You know what I'm saying. It was great. We're good. No worries and you're sneaking out wasn't required. I won't be stalking you, I swear."

The thought of Ophelia Finlay stalking anyone was so damn foreign I would have laughed if I could. A woman like her didn't need to stalk a man. She needed to be concerned with being stalked herself.

"I wasn't worried you'd be stalking me," I confirmed although I knew she'd been trying to lighten the mood.

She took a drink of her coffee. The fullness of her lips was distracting. I needed to be leaving. Watching her drink coffee and being turned on by it wasn't helping matters. I was not good for her. It was that simple. After last night, she had to know it too.

"Leave, Eli. I know you want to go. Just don't think I'm expecting anything more from you. That wasn't what last night was about."

There it was. She wanted me gone. This was what I expected, but a large portion of me had hoped she'd try to get me to stay. When I was near her, life was better . . . no, it was more than better. Seeing her was worth waking up for. It had been so long since I had a reason to open my eyes and live. That was all fantasy though. I could never act on it.

I dropped my arms and straightened. Leave, just leave. That's all I had to do. What I would do for her sake.

"Thanks for dinner," I said not sure what the proper goodbye was here.

"Thanks for eating it," she replied with an amused smirk.

The tacos had been good. I'd told her that last night already so I didn't say it again just to prolong the inevitable. I made my way to the door. We'd said everything else. Or almost everything else. I paused with my hand on the doorknob. Then figured what the hell. I had one last thing to say.

Glancing back over my shoulder my gaze met hers. She hadn't moved from her position, but she'd been watching me leave. "The sex was amazing," I told her.

"I agree," she replied. Her pleased grin made me want to smile in return, but I didn't. "Scale from one to ten?" she asked me.

That one was easy. I finally gave into the smile that tugged at my lips. "Best I ever had," I replied then without giving her a chance to say more, I opened the door and left. I didn't need to know if I was the best she'd ever had. Or how I ranked on a scale from one to ten.

Honestly, I didn't like being reminded other men had been inside her and that itself was reason enough for me to get the hell out of here. Too deep. Too easily. I forgot my past when I was with her and I never needed to forget. It was who I had become.

She didn't call out to me or follow me. It should have been a relief instead of a disappointment. When I got on my bike and cranked it up, I glanced to the kitchen window of the flat. She stood there watching me. I could easily stay right here and look at her for the rest of my life. Seeing what I couldn't have but wanting to be near her.

She was everything I wish I'd known before.

Chapter Eleven

❤ OPHELIA FINLAY ❤

JUNE 07 / 7:05 PM

THE KERRINGTON CLUB was a part of my life. It wasn't just Rosemary Beach's country club . . . it was a second home as I was growing up. Every big event in my family happened at the Kerrington Club. Weddings, baby showers, birthday parties, cotillion, coming out balls, prom, tennis lessons, and any other event my parents' circle of friends could dream up. It was always at the club.

Tonight was a first for all of us though. This would be the first movie premier held at the Kerrington Club. Woods Kerrington was the president of the club and his middle son, Blaze, had landed his first main role in a movie. Upon his request, there was a private viewing for friends and family at the club tonight exactly one week before its box office release.

If it wasn't for the fact my boss, landlord, and best friend wasn't Blaze's sister-in-law, I would have probably spent my evening at home. Not that I wasn't happy for Blaze. I was. Truly, I was. But this was not my kind of event. The getting dressed up was the first annoying thing about it. Black tie seemed a bit much. The cameras going off in our faces as we arrived was even more against my guidelines for a successful Friday night.

I much preferred Netflix and ice cream. Mint chocolate chip to be exact. Also, my pajamas were my choice of attire. Instead, I was in a black cocktail dress that I'd worn three years ago to Phoenix's graduation party . . . at guess where? The club. I figured no one would remember it. I also didn't expect to be in any photos considering I wasn't very close to Blaze, at least since we'd gotten past puberty. I also wasn't family.

Mom had called to ask if I wanted to ride with them. I knew she was worried about my sudden reclusiveness. The past few weeks I had worked and stayed home. Sundays had been the only time they saw me. I hadn't even called to check on Phoenix or sent her another text message for her to ignore. She was avoiding me and that was fine. Dad had said she was doing okay and that's all I needed to know. Honestly, I wanted to hear her voice, but I wasn't going to dwell on it.

Mom had been disappointed when I said I'd drive myself. Having my own vehicle meant I could escape when I wanted to. My parents would stay because Blaze's parents were some of their closest friends. Dad was also a board member at the Kerrington Club. It was expected for him to be there. I, however, could slip on out when I was ready.

I knew Mom had hoped I was bringing a date when I had declined her offer. I could hear the unasked question in her tone, but I ignored it. No reason to let her down further. My invitation had said I could bring a plus one. I had RSVPed without that option. I had no one I was interested in taking. The funk I was in had to do with a man if I was honest with myself. So I was taking my mood on Eli Hardy out on all the male population. Probably wasn't healthy, but I was doing it anyway.

Eli had left my apartment the morning after our mind-blowing night of sex and not called, texted, or shown up at my loft. Not one word. When he'd left after telling me I was the best he'd ever had, the smile on my face that day had been ridiculously bright. Even Lila Kate mentioned my mood. The next day I was still feeling the glow, but as the second day came to an end and I'd checked my phone a million times for a text or missed call from him, I started to get that maybe it wouldn't come.

A week went by and I knew he wasn't going to contact me again. The best he ever had comment had been bullshit. Something he could say to ease the fact he was running off and not coming back. I'd been a fling. I hadn't ever been a fling for a man. Sure, I'd had one fling in college, but I had chosen him as a fling after a bad breakup. He hadn't chosen me as a fling.

Eli Hardy had not been a fling for me. I'd wanted to have sex with him and after the experience, I had wanted more of it. Not just the sex. More of him. Eli had not felt the same way. I was ashamed to admit I had spent hours thinking over what I'd done wrong. How I had turned him off being around me. I could only come to the conclusion he wasn't interested in me. I wasn't his type. That had caused me to eat more mint chocolate chip ice cream than my hips needed.

The valet line at the club was longer than normal, but then for private parties it always was. If I hadn't decided to wear the six-inch heels I had on, I would just park and walk. I waited in the line instead to save my feet. Besides, it was more time I didn't have to go inside and pretend like I wanted to be there. I was sure Blaze's movie was great. I'd seen the preview on television more than once. It looked good. But the socializing I wasn't crazy about. My mother studying me and trying to figure out my mood was also a reason to dread this. She wasn't pushy, but she would worry.

Two cars ahead of me I recognized as Nate's newest Range Rover. I hadn't realized it until I saw Nate step out though. I watched as the backdoors both opened while the valet was opening Bliss's door for her. I didn't have time to be confused by the back doors or a moment to let it sink in that someone had come with them until I saw the dark thick heavy curls and the skin-tight red dress that barely hit mid-thigh. My eyes were on Saffron Corbin. I was surprised she'd managed to get an invitation. Bliss nor Nate cared for her much. She often made scenes in public places. My gaze swung from that side of the car to the other. My throat tightened and I gripped the steering wheel so tightly my knuckles went white. Eli Hardy was closing the door he'd gotten out of, dressed in a tux. My first thought was he filled one out much better than the last time I'd seen him in one. My second thought was he was who had brought Saffron. She was his date.

A few choice names ran through my head as he walked over to stand beside her. Nate said something to him and he and Saffron made their way toward the entrance. I watched them, not sure what I was feeling. Shock, disappointment, anger . . . I wasn't sure which one was the strongest. Until he placed a hand on her back as she entered the club. The word, "motherfucking bastard," came from my lips and I knew then it was definitely anger that was winning. I was pissed. My stomach was in knots as well which meant the anger had to do with hurt. I could admit that. But only to myself.

Saffron Corbin, seriously? Of all the people in that stupid town he lived in, he chose Saffron as his date? Wasn't she a stripper or something? I'd heard she got arrested with strippers in a pool. I couldn't remember details because I hadn't really listened to the story when it was being told. But it was one of many about her. She was a slut.

If that was what Eli wanted then fine. I didn't want him in
my bed again. I didn't want him near me again. I sure as hell didn't
want to speak to him again. As if this night wasn't bad enough,
he had to show up here and bring a freaking date. The hurt was
quickly being drowned out by anger and disgust.

By the time my car rolled up to the valet, I was giving myself
a pep talk. Calming down, getting over it, because I was about to
walk in there and smile, pretend like I owned the place, and not
look his way once. He'd regret this one day. I wasn't sure when
but he would. Because I might have been moody the past few
weeks, but tonight I was about to play a better role than Blaze
Kerrington ever thought of. I was a female on a mission.

I stepped out of my car when the door was opened by the
valet and smiled at him. I was practicing and it was working. He
flushed. That probably was an unfair way to gauge the effective-
ness of my smile. The kid was probably eighteen years old. But
I felt better none the less.

Eli Hardy better watch out. I wasn't worried about Saffron.
She'd done nothing wrong. It hadn't been her I'd cooked for then
had wild sex with on my couch. She wasn't the one to walk out
and never call again. No, Saffron was not the enemy. I wasn't vin-
dictive with women. It had never been my way to handle things.
Even when my boyfriend in college had been caught cheating
with another girl. One I knew. I hadn't been mean to her. She
hadn't been the one I was dating. Sure, she was okay with dating
a cheater, but that was her issue, not mine.

No, a Finlay didn't attack everyone in their wake. They went
after who had hurt them and they made them regret it. Except
possibly Phoenix, she'd destroy them all. Female included. Regardless, Eli Hardy was about to get a taste of how bad it was to
screw around with a Finlay. We weren't weak and we didn't give
sympathy where it wasn't due.

Chapter Twelve

~ELI HARDY~

JUNE 07 / 7:27 PM

"CRUZ IS GOING to regret having an invitation sent to me when his brother jumps out a motherfucking window," I muttered to Bliss as we stood inside the large ballroom area we'd been directed to.

Bliss cut her eyes at me. "I don't think this place has a window high enough for him to truly do damage," she whispered back. "He may just go drown himself in the fancy pool they have here."

Nate was talking to Woods Kerrington who had been standing at the entrance greeting guests. Woods was Cruz and Blaze's father. He also owned the club. His grandfather had built the place. Bliss and I hadn't grown up in this world with these people and although we had been raised in a wealthier lifestyle than average, this was on another realm for us. The one percenters filled the place and it made me want a beer and my jeans. Too uptight of a crowd for me.

I glanced over to my right to see Saffron was still working on getting Blaze's attention. He was the reason she was here. I'd been going to come because I was selfish and wanted to see Ophelia. Saffron did some detective work and found out I had an invite. She'd worn me down for a week until I agreed to bring her. Besides, it gave Holland, her twin sister, a Friday night free of any Saffron clean up. Typically, Holland had to pick up Saffron from a bar or bail her out of jail on weekend nights.

I wasn't related to the Corbins, but they were like family. I'd always seen the twins as I did my sisters. Although if one of my sisters acted the way Saffron did, I'd lock her in the attic until she was thirty. The girl was exhausting.

Blaze had a crowd around him and what looked like a date of his own hooked on his right arm. Good luck with that, Saffron, I thought. Not that it would stop her. She would see the other girl as a challenge. The other girl would possibly lose. Depended on how this upper-crust worked and if Saffron could handle the different tax bracket.

"Come on, we're going over to the table Woods said was reserved for us. We stay in here for drinks and mingling then the people from the production company will speak and so will Blaze before we exit to go to the theatre," Bliss explained to me. I grabbed Saffron's elbow to get her attention then nodded my head toward Nate and Bliss who were now walking to the far left of the room.

I didn't wait for Saffron to follow me because she'd stall if I did. She was not going to want to move farther away from Blaze's line of vision.

"Can you introduce me to him?" Saffron asked, falling into step beside me. Her heels added to her five-nine height putting her at my eye level. Which made it easier to talk to her and not need to lean down and get closer to her. I wasn't here to get cozied up to Saffron. I knew the real reason I was here and avoiding the fact was pointless.

"Eventually," I replied. "I need a drink and he appears busy at the moment."

Saffron sighed a little too dramatically. "Fine. I need a drink too."

"You're not old enough to drink," I replied. "She wasn't going to get drunk at this event and leave me to deal with her.

"I'm almost twenty-one!" she said defensively.

"You're not drinking." The hard edge to my voice thankfully shut her up. For now at least. I knew she didn't back down easy . . . or ever.

Nate stopped at a table and pulled out a chair for Bliss. Once Bliss was seated, I did the same for Saffron placing her beside Bliss. If anyone could put up with Saffron, it was Bliss. She had patience with Saffron. I had, once, before things had changed me. I'd lost that patience this past year. Saffron was a walking time bomb. Her father wasn't going to be able to clean up the disaster she left in her wake forever. One day something would happen that she'd have to truly pay for. Regret would be a real word for her then. And only after she lived through that would she have the hope of changing.

"There's Ophelia," Bliss said cheerfully beside me.

Just her name and my spirits lifted. Fuck me. All the times I'd fought my urge to text her or call her. To show up at her place, and here I was willingly putting myself in her presence. For what? Torture possibly? I had given up on my resolve to not see her again. This opportunity gave me a chance and I took it.

I was going to look. I couldn't not look. I was too damn weak not to look at her. Turning my head in the direction Bliss was looking, I saw her standing by the waterfall of what I thought was possibly champagne. A flute was in her hand as she smiled up at some man I didn't know. That smile, her voice, and the way her pale blonde hair stood out like a halo against the black dress she was wearing, the combination would have any male spellbound.

Instead of the nightmares I'd endured the past six months since the night with Ophelia I'd had none. When I dreamed it was of her. Just like being in her presence soothed me, the thought of her did the same thing in my dreams. Her power over me was a weakness I couldn't accept because I wasn't good for her. My soul was too damaged.

Ophelia was nothing like Alice. She was honesty, light, and beauty. The darkness in Alice had been masked but not forever. By the time I saw the traces of what she was hiding underneath Alice's outward appearance it was too late. I loved her. The darkness hadn't been her fault. She'd suffered abuse as a young girl. It left a mark that I had stupidly thought I could heal. But the marks left on her life had made it impossible. I couldn't save her from herself. Just like I hadn't been able to save our child from her.

The deep sharp edge that felt like a blade ripping through my chest came with the memory. As it always did. I swallowed hard and forced my breathing to remain even. Here was not the time to think of that. But it was always there waiting to unleash its power over me. The horror that would forever haunt me. The reason why keeping my distance from Ophelia Finlay was important. I was irreparable and I knew it.

As if she could hear her name in my thoughts, her head turned. Ophelia's gaze traveled over me as if I were invisible. Then it met Bliss's and she smiled. No, she fucking beamed a smile so bright it made everyone else in the room dim in comparison. Ophelia returned her attention to the man in front of her and I saw him look disappointed he was losing her as she then made her way toward us.

Correction, made her way toward Bliss and Nate. It was clear she was not acknowledging me. Her eyes looked through me as if I weren't here at all. My seat might as well have been vacant. Bliss stood up to greet her and Ophelia hugged her then did the same to her brother who had yet to sit down as he was standing talking to a man I didn't know. The man greeted her and she smiled at him too.

"You look stunning," Bliss said to her.

"Thank you and as always you are gorgeous," Ophelia replied graciously.

Bliss then introduced Saffron saying she wasn't sure if they had met before.

Ophelia gave Saffron that same bright smile and said she remembered her from the wedding, but they hadn't officially met. I watched it all take place in front of me as I was ignored. She didn't glance my way or act like I was sitting here. Bliss had no reason to mention my presence because there was no introduction needed. Ophelia then noticed someone in the direction of the entrance and that fucking smile returned.

"I'll come back later, I need to go say hello. Y'all be sure to go get some of that champagne. It's delicious," she added then flashed Saffron one last smile to let her know she was included in that comment before walking away with the slight sway to her hips as if she owned the world. I didn't doubt for a second that she just might, in fact, own it all.

Once she was gone, I felt Bliss's eyes on me. She'd not acted differently when Ophelia was standing here, but she'd noticed the slight in my direction from her. I could go get something to drink or deal with Bliss now. I had a feeling this evening was going to go on with Ophelia pretending I wasn't here, so I went ahead and faced Bliss. Her curiosity would get the best of her eventually and she'd demand an answer.

I swung my gaze to meet Bliss's. She was frowning as she

studied me. I just stared at her waiting. She'd ask me after she was done trying to figure it out herself.

"What did you do?" she asked me finally.

There were so many answers to that. I could ask her to be more specific, but we'd been best friends since the nursery. There was no point dragging this out.

"I can honestly tell you I'm not exactly sure. But I'll find out before we leave."

That was as close to the truth as I could give her. Because to be honest, the way we had left things seemed as if she was good with it. The way she'd just blatantly ignored me said otherwise.

Bliss glared at me then. "Oh, you know. I don't believe that for a second." The disapproval in her didn't go unnoticed. Saffron who had been preoccupied eye stalking Blaze snapped her attention back to the table.

"What happened?" she asked, suddenly interested in something other than the movie star.

Bliss looked at Saffron and changed her angry warning scowl she'd sent me to a smile. "Apparently, nothing," she told Saffron. Bliss may be mad at me for unknown reasons to both of us but a lifetime of being two against the rest of the Sea Breeze offspring remained in effect.

Saffron was not easily swayed though. She turned to look at me. "Is it about the way Ophelia ignored you?" she asked.

I shot Bliss my own annoyed glance this time. If she'd not said anything, then Saffron wouldn't have heard her.

Bliss looked slightly sorry but not enough so that she was letting this go. She was mad at me for Ophelia's sake. Even if she didn't know why. Women.

Nate turned to Bliss, his conversation over. "Do you want a drink?" he asked her.

She swung her glare from me to her husband who she gazed

at lovingly. "Champagne would be great," she told him.

He bent to kiss her then straightened up. I thought he was going to leave to go get the drink when he turned his gaze to me. "Whatever you did, good luck. You're gonna need it. My sister shows no mercy." The pleased gleam in his eyes was as close to a warning as I was going to get from him. Then he left to go get Bliss's drink.

I didn't meet Bliss's gaze again.

"So you did make Ophelia mad!" Saffron said as if this were juicy gossip. "Oh, wait, there he goes. I'll be back," she then added with a waggle of her eyebrows jumping up and strutting off in the direction of Blaze Kerrington.

At least she was over talking about Ophelia. I wouldn't have to escape just yet. I stood to go get myself a drink. I sure as hell needed one. With a sideways glance in the direction Ophelia had gone, I found her easily enough since she made others pale in comparison when she entered a room. She was talking with yet another man I didn't know and the grin she was giving him had his rapt attention. I doubted he knew what had hit him.

Ophelia may have acted like she thought nothing of our night together, but she'd thought something. It was clear she was angry with me. I hadn't called and she was not okay with that. She'd expected me to. I wanted to. God how I'd wanted to.

Coming tonight had been a bad idea.

Chapter Thirteen

♥ OPHELIA FINLAY ♥

JUNE 07 / 9:41 PM

BEFORE THE CREDITS began to roll, I slipped out the back door to the theatre. I was done with pretending like I was happy to be here and that I enjoyed flirting with all the men I'd spoken to. The movie had been a reprieve from that but now it was over, I was afraid a couple of the guys I'd talked to might want to talk some more. I knew them all, of course. Once Bay Howington had even been my boyfriend in the eighth grade. I'd broken up with him at thirteen and wasn't interested in going down that road again.

They were guys I chose strategically because I knew Eli wouldn't know them and because I felt comfortable enough to talk to them. I hadn't counted on a couple getting the wrong idea. Regardless, I had been a manipulative jealous bitch and now I needed to get out of here before it got worse.

Just as I opened the door leading to the stairs that went back up to the main level, a hand touched my elbow and I jumped with a squeal of surprise. The dimly lit hallway had been empty and everyone else was still inside the theatre. Spinning around to see who had touched me, my words of scolding for scaring me half to death I saw Bay attempting a charming smile. He may possibly consider it sexy. I deserved this.

He was close and I hadn't been expecting to see him or anyone else during my escape. "Jesus, Bay! What are you doing out here lurking in the hallway?" I snapped, moving back away from him. I wasn't in the mood to pretend to flirt anymore. Bay needed to go back inside and forget my earlier friendliness.

"I didn't mean to startle you. I just saw you leave and figured if I wanted to catch you before you left. Maybe we could go get drinks or something." The way he said "something" made me inwardly cringe. I'd chosen poorly when I'd picked Bay as one of the men to give extra attention to tonight. I deserved this. I really did. However, it still annoyed me. My asking about his mother and listening to him go on about his very brief marriage hadn't exactly been romantic conversation.

"I'm tired and ready to go home," I replied, hoping he left it at that. He shifted his arrogant stance and it moved him a few inches closer to me. I, in return, back up just as much. We weren't going to get cozy out here. I was trying to leave. Surely, that was obvious.

"Maybe tomorrow evening then? I'd like to reconnect. It's been too long." He had dropped his voice an octave. I would not be rude and roll my eyes no matter how badly I wanted to. This was the Bay from high school. The one who thought he was king. He hadn't changed at all. Not even when his wife left him for another man. His ego was still going strong.

"No, I don't think so. I'm busy and not looking to connect with anyone." That was blunt. I could have been softer with my refusal, but I doubted Bay would allow me to be anything but blunt to shake him loose.

He leaned in with a creepy smile. "Sure didn't seem that way earlier."

No, it hadn't. Because I'd been busy acting like a jealous female. Ignoring Eli would have been sufficient. Why had I decided to flirt?

"Bay, I was just being friendly. I want to go now, so if you'll excuse me," I said and started to turn when he reached out and took my hand in his. I tried to snatch it back, but he held firm.

"She said she was leaving. Let go of her hand." Eli's deep voice wasn't loud, but the threat in it was clear. I swung my glare from Bay to Eli.

He was standing there with his hands in his pockets and his eyes on me.

"Who the fuck are you?" Bay asked annoyed and suddenly sounding less sure of himself.

Eli didn't spare him a glance. He continued to look at me.

"Thanks, Eli. But I have this under control." I was annoyed that he thought he needed to rescue me. I tugged again at my hand and this time it was released. I didn't need to stand here and speak to either of the two men. Turning, I headed back to the stairs without another word.

"I'll call you," Bay said as if he had my phone number. I knew he did not. I didn't respond.

"She didn't ask you to follow her." Eli's tone had darkened. I could keep going and ignore this, but I didn't. I paused and glanced back. Bay had, in fact, started to follow me. Seriously? Was he that desperate?

I turned my focus to Eli. "Thank you, but I told you I had this under control."

"So you can see me now?" he asked as he lifted one eyebrow

in a mocking way that pissed me off.

"I don't know what you are talking about," I said with a haughty lift of my shoulders then shot Bay an annoyed glare. "I am not interested. Leave me alone, Bay." That seemed to get through his thick skull or at least hit his ego hard enough that he didn't say more. Instead he gave me an annoyed glare of his own before heading back to the theatre.

I waited until the door closed behind him before I spun around and headed back up the stairs. I hoped that Eli would say something more or at least try to stop me because I was weak when it came to him. He said nothing and I was instantly let down even if I didn't want to care as I climbed the stairs. It was about the fifth step that I realized he may not have tried to stop me, but he was following me.

I managed to glare at him over my shoulder. "Where are you going?"

He looked behind him as if I were talking to someone else then looked back at me. I was not amused. He pointed at his chest. "Are you speaking to me?" he asked.

I rolled my eyes and returned to my escape up the stairs. He continued with following me. Once I reached the main floor, I made sure to walk with purpose but give a good sway to my hips while I was at it. Might as well give him something to look at.

I could only hear the clicking of my heels on the marble floor and when I was close to the door that led back out to the valet, I chanced a look over my shoulder. He was there several steps behind me but following me still. I was happy about it and that made me a complete loser. Where was my pride? He had left my house after sex and I'd not heard a word from him since. Then he had shown up with Saffron Corbin tonight! He knew I'd be here. Yet he brought her.

"What do you want?" I demanded. He had no reason to be

following me even if a large part of me was happy that he was doing so.

"To talk to you," he said simply.

Damn him. Why now? Because of Bay? I shouldn't allow him to talk. Not now. Maybe a couple weeks ago that would have been a nice idea. But he didn't want to talk to me then. He shouldn't get to talk to me now. What could he say to fix things? Nothing. He had said enough when he said nothing at all. I was about to say that then snapped my mouth shut and sighed with enough force behind it to cause a dramatic rise and fall of my shoulders.

"What do you want to talk about?" I asked him. Although we were the only people here right now, that would soon change and we both knew it. I wasn't going to offer to go to a more private location. His time was limited.

"We could start with why I was invisible tonight," he suggested as if he was clueless.

"That's what you want to talk about?" I asked then spun around to leave again. I had hoped he had some groveling, explaining, anything else in mind than acting like I had no reason to ignore him.

"Ophelia, wait. I'm trying to figure out what I've done." His words were so freaking sincere, I paused. I should go outside, ask for my car, and leave. I'd accomplished what I'd set out to do tonight. He had been ignored and he didn't like it. Good for me. It was time to leave. But I didn't.

"Where's your date?" I snapped at him. Then decided to rub that in. "Oh, wait, she's with Blaze." I'd seen Saffron use all her flirting skills on Blaze tonight and I'd give it to her, she handled him like a pro. There was no man on earth that loved himself more than Blaze. The way Saffron had worked him was impressive.

Eli smirked then. "Yeah, she is. I owe him a great deal of gratitude for relieving me of her."

I frowned, annoyed with his reply. I'd used that one on him in my head about five times tonight while sitting watching the movie and imagining a confrontation like this one. Eli would look embarrassed and apologize. I wouldn't forgive him. He was messing up my scenario. He shouldn't be happy his date dumped him.

"You wanted your date to leave you for another man?" I asked him incredulously. That was doubtful.

He nodded slowly. "Have you ever spent a few minutes in Saffron's company?" he shot back at me.

I hadn't. Not really. I shook my head.

"You'd understand if you had."

That confused me which only added to more confusion he'd left in his wake since last I'd seen him. All Eli Hardy seemed to do was confuse me. About everything. I didn't like being confused. I wish I didn't like him. Damn him.

"Why did you bring her if she annoys you?" I wanted something to make sense.

He ran a hand through his hair looking exasperated. "Because she knew I had an invite and begged me. She wanted to meet Blaze. She was annoying the fuck out of me about it. I gave in," he said this with no emotion then added, "Can you tell me why you ignored me all night?"

He'd brought Saffron to meet Blaze. That took some wind out of my sails. At least with my explanation. Sure, he hadn't called me or texted, but I had ultimately been angry because I'd been jealous that he was here with her. I would have been pissed if he'd been here with anyone.

"You had forgotten me. I simply reacted in turn," I admitted. It was vulnerable of me and if he hadn't told me why he'd brought Saffron, I may not have given him the truth. But the explanation came out before I could think it through. I might have sounded less petty if I had been less blunt.

"You think I forgot you existed?" he asked, his brows drawn together in disbelief.

"What else was I supposed to think?" I wanted to say more. Remind him he hadn't called or texted. But I had a little pride left. I was holding onto that. I wasn't going to spell it out for him.

"When I left, you seemed fine with us leaving things like that. You didn't act like you expected more. Was I wrong?" he asked me.

Was he wrong? That was his concern? Really? This man could not be that dense. I was also done talking to him about this. If he was going to be dumb then so be it.

"No, Eli. You were right. Now, if you'll excuse me, I want to get out of here before they all come upstairs." I didn't smile. I didn't say goodbye. I just got the hell out of that building. The head valet knew me and gave a nod to let me know he was having my car brought around.

I thought Eli may join me. When a few minutes went by and the door didn't open behind me, I knew he wasn't going to. The sight of my car meant my silent hope he'd try harder was in vain. The man had no clue or he didn't want to act as if he did. Whatever the reason, I was done.

I tipped the valet then climbed into my car and drove away.

Glad to be gone.

Sad that it was done.

Chapter Fourteen

~ELI HARDY~

JUNE 07 / 10:39 PM

"*Y*OU SURE YOU want me to just drop you off and not wait? Because I know my sister and there is a ninety-nine percent chance you'll be paying Uber to drive your ass back to Sea Breeze and that won't be cheap." Nate sounded serious when he warned me. He'd laughed when I told him to take me to Ophelia's. Then when he realized I wasn't joking he seemed more concerned.

"Does Uber even serve this area?" Bliss asked, not sounding as if she was liking the idea of me being dropped off either. "Maybe you should go see if Ophelia will let you in before we leave."

I didn't want them to sit out here while I went to the door. I wasn't so sure Ophelia was going to let me in either, but if they were here to witness this, she may send me packing easier. I'd let her leave earlier without saying more because it was a conversation I wanted to have in private.

We'd had to wait to find out if Saffron needed a ride or not. Bliss and Nate had been ready to leave, but Saffron wasn't concerned with anyone but herself. It had taken more time than necessary. My concern now was that Ophelia could be asleep. It had taken too damn long to get out of there.

"It's fine. Y'all go," I said, opening the car door and climbing out.

"Don't say I didn't warn you," Nate drawled trying not to sound amused for Bliss's sake. She wasn't amused at all and wanted to wait. I could see it in her expression.

I stepped up on the sidewalk and waited until they drove off. They didn't need to witness this. Once they were gone, I headed for the door and rang the bell to the loft. There was a chance she was asleep and if she was, I figured I'd Uber to Destin and get a hotel there for the night. Then try again tomorrow.

Until I talked to her, I wasn't going back to Sea Breeze. I knew I should let this go and forget it. But I couldn't. Seeing her again tonight solidified that I couldn't stay away from her. I didn't want to. Even if it was for her best interest that I keep my distance, I couldn't fucking do it.

"Why are you here, Eli?" Her voice came over the speaker connected to the doorbell.

"To talk," I replied, hoping I didn't have to do it over the damn video camera she had attached to her door.

"We talked. What else is there to say?" Her voice was raspy and I wondered if I had woken her up.

"A lot . . . a lot of shit I should have said before."

She didn't respond to that right away. I wasn't sure if she was cutting me off or if she'd fallen back asleep. When the seconds turned into a minute then two, I was about to ring again and start my talk right here on this damn sidewalk.

But a light came on inside just before I rang the bell a second time and I saw her coming toward the door through the windows. I relaxed some but not completely. She still may not be planning on letting me in. Our talk could very well take place right here with me standing outside and her inside the doorway. It was something though.

I heard the lock click free and then the door opened more slowly than necessary. As if she was debating on shutting it and locking it again. All that blonde hair I was so fascinated with was in a messy knot on top of her head. The makeup from earlier was scrubbed free and her face was natural yet still stunning. The oversized sweatshirt and boxer shorts she was wearing were her chosen sleep attire, so she'd been in bed or about to get into bed when I arrived.

"Come inside," she said with no enthusiasm. It was clear she didn't want to talk to me, but she was going to do it against her better judgment.

I stepped inside and waited as she locked the door again then I followed her toward the door that led to the loft. She said nothing as we headed up the stairs. No questions or warnings to be quick. I wished I knew what she was thinking so I'd have some idea about how to handle this. How much truth to tell her. If I should explain it all . . . although I didn't think I could.

Now I was inside I wasn't sure what to say first. My goal had been to talk to her until she understood but how did I do that exactly. What did she want me to say? I had spent the past couple of weeks thinking she had considered what we'd done a good time. Nothing more. Until she had acted like I was invisible tonight, I'd believed it had been only me affected by our time together.

She walked over to the overstuffed blue chair that sat across from the sofa and sank down into it then stared at me. "You're here. Now what else did you need to say?" She was matter of fact. No smiles. None of the flirty behavior she'd displayed in the past.

I hadn't expected it of course. She was angry with me.

I moved over to the sofa and sat down on the edge, letting my elbows rest on my knees as I sat forward. This wasn't something I wanted to appear relaxed about. I wasn't fucking relaxed so there was no need to appear as if I was. When I walked out of her door the last time believing this was over had been foolish. I had wanted it to be for her sake, but after tonight, I wouldn't be able to save her from me. Her pull was too damn strong.

"I've thought of little else but you since I was here last," I admitted, and her bored expression didn't budge. I shouldn't have expected it to. Her brother had warned me already. He would know her better than anyone. My telling her I thought about her all the time didn't change the fact I'd not contacted her. That was how she saw it.

"When I left that morning, I was confused about the way I was feeling. It wasn't something I expected. Just like I hadn't come here to see you expecting us to . . ." I paused, unsure which word would describe it adequately. I didn't want to cheapen what had happened between us on this sofa.

"Fuck for hours," she said with no trace of a smile. Not even an icy one.

I wasn't going to agree with her description because I considered it more than fucking. She'd gotten inside me in a way no one else had. I knew that now and I was learning to accept it. "Not the description I'd give it," I told her, not letting her coldness stop me from being honest. "That night surprised me. You surprised me and the connection . . . it was . . . I hadn't expected it. When I left, I thought it had been a fun night where you were concerned and I had to deal with it and move on." I stopped again, making sure I thought through my next words. Blurting shit out never worked well for me. I was a thinker and that was not something that tattoos, tragedy and horror couldn't change. Words couldn't be taken back. Once they were spoken, they remained. Never forgotten and seldom forgiven. I knew that too well. The words I chose to use with Ophelia would not be ones I regretted. I could at least protect her from my words even if I was not going to protect her from getting close to me.

"You were standing in my room ready to bolt without a word when I woke up, Eli," she reminded me. As if that answered everything. Maybe to a woman it did, but I wasn't a female and I had never been able to understand the opposite sex. I'd failed so many damn times at guessing what they meant measured beside what they had said, I was giving up on that hope.

"I was deciding on waking you or leaving you a note. Not because I didn't want to speak to you but because you were sleeping peacefully. There was no sneaking out in my decision. I'd just had the best sex of my life and I didn't know the next step or if there was a next step."

I knew more had to be said, but from that explanation, the ice in her glare thawed some. Just a tiny bit. Not enough by a long shot but it was softer by a degree or two. Telling her all of the truth I could was the only way to deal with the situation we were in. If I couldn't stay away from her, then I had to do all I could to get her forgiveness.

"I left under the impression you wanted to continue as things were which was . . . hell, I don't know. Until that weekend, I'd barely spoken to you enough to call you a friend. But I need you to understand that not a day has gone by since I left here that I haven't thought about you. That I didn't want to pick up the phone and call you."

There was the fucking truth. One I should have kept to myself.

Frustration crossed her beautiful features. "Then why didn't you?"

Because I was trying to protect you from me. Because I am

not a man who can love, not anymore. Because my addiction to you will never be enough for us to last. Craving someone is not the same as loving them. All of those were reasons I shouldn't even be sitting here. I said none of that though. I was too selfish.

"I didn't think you wanted me to." I stopped myself before I blurted out more and held her gaze. If she looked close enough, she'd see the darkness inside me. She needed to know I was too fucked up now to ever be what she was looking for.

"I don't sleep around, and I don't have casual sex. Before you, I hadn't slept with a man in over a year. Sure, I'd had some wine, but I wasn't drunk that night. I knew what I was doing, and I trusted you enough to do it. I wouldn't have done either of those things if I didn't want to see you more." She said the last part like she was confused by why it was even being said. I knew my vagueness was confusing. My secrets would be unfair to keep from her if I was going to do this. If I was going to give in to wanting to be near her and feel peace again. She was the only person who could make me smile or feel like laughing. When I thought I'd never want to do either again, she'd given me a reason to want to without even realizing it. With her, I had a freedom but what did she get in return? Nothing. She got nothing.

"There's some emotional damage that I don't think I can ever heal from. I'm not going to be able to let someone in completely. You deserve to be given it all. I can't be that man. But I want to be near you. I crave your presence and that's all I know. It's selfish that I came here. Asking for anything with you is fucking selfish." The words came tumbling out of me like a motherfucking truth serum.

She uncrossed her legs and sat up straighter. There was no sign of the earlier frost in her eyes. That had vanished as quickly as I'd blurted out the shit I hadn't thought through. Instead of looking confused by what I'd said, she appeared thoughtful and poised. I knew she was turning it over and thinking it through. Just watching her was like being given a small gift. Her beauty could make a man forget every dark corner of his life. That either made her dangerous or an angel. I wasn't sure which.

"I'd like a chance to decide what is and isn't good for me," she told me. "I don't need to know what secrets you're keeping that make you feel as if you are broken in some way. Not yet at least. Right now we can go slowly. Test the waters. See if this mutual attraction we are both feeling is worth fighting whatever obstacles lay ahead."

She made it sound so simple. Easy even. I was willing to agree to anything if I could keep her for awhile. I knew forever wasn't going to happen. Nothing was simple or easy about the truth. I wasn't the kind of man who could hold onto Ophelia Finlay. If I had been whole, she'd still grow tired of me. She was excitement, beauty, energy all tangled together perfectly in one stunning female. I'd thought so the first time I'd met her. Even then I'd known she was to be admired from afar.

I'd never been able to hold onto a woman before. Believing I could hold onto one as magnificent as this one would make me a fool. I would reserve my heart or what was left of it. But the rest of me she already had. Without her asking for it, I'd handed it over the last time I was here.

"Okay," I agreed. Only an idiot would turn down an offer like that.

Chapter Fifteen

♥ OPHELIA FINLAY ♥

JUNE 08 / 6:59 AM

HE WAS BEAUTIFUL when he slept. I wondered if he knew that. Had another woman told him before? His lashes were so long and dark in contrast with his blonde hair. His lips full and his jawline wide and strong. Which was what made the other features appear masculine. Otherwise he'd be too pretty to be a man. The wide expanse of his shoulders that weren't covered up by the blankets also made those perfect features manly. I wanted to reach out and stroke his shoulders and tattoo-covered arm, but I refrained. Mostly because I didn't want to wake him and also because I was still so unsure about us.

Yes, he was in my bed, but we hadn't had sex last night. When we had finished talking, I'd asked him to stay. Then shown him where the towels were in the bathroom so he could shower. There was a pair of Cruz's athletic shorts left here from when Lila Kate still lived here. I kept forgetting to give them to her. Last night they had come in handy for Eli. I'd laid them out on the bathroom counter and explained why I had a pair of men's shorts.

He'd walked out of the bathroom into my bedroom and I was already in bed. I had pulled back the covers for him to join me. He had without a pause and then tucked me against his chest. Nothing more. No kissing. No talking. It had been so warm and comfortable I'd been asleep within minutes. Little time to think about much more.

It felt silly to think I couldn't touch him if I wanted to. We'd been close all night. It just seemed too soon. After last night's talk, this should be clear but in reality, it wasn't. Or I was just being weird about it all which I was good at. Then there was the little issue with my wanting to have sex with him again . . . like right now.

His breathing remained deep and slow. He wasn't waking up and I needed to use the bathroom. As quietly as I could, I slipped out of bed and went to handle my morning necessities. This way my teeth would be brushed before he woke up so that was a plus. No morning breath to worry about. I also ran a brush through my hair to get out the tangles before tiptoeing back into the room then toward the kitchen to make coffee. Saturday morning toddler "princess camp" classes started at nine. Which meant I had to be down there getting lights turned on, stocking the waters, making sure the dance supply store had all the merchandise displayed and answering the phone by eight-thirty.

Coffee was required first. Then another cup before I was truly functional. Otherwise, I was groggy and often grumpy. I started the espresso machine and then turned the coffee pot on. Monday through Sunday I needed two shots of espresso in my coffee. I realize that's every day of the week, but it made me a nicer person.

I turned my head to stare at the fridge and wondered if it was overkill to make breakfast for Eli. Was it rude if I didn't? I had stayed single so long, I was terrible at having men over. I'd forgotten what was the polite thing to do. I doubted Eli expected me to cook him anything but was that the point?

While I went about fixing my espresso, I asked myself did I like Eli enough to want him around a lot? Yes. Was I happy this morning waking up in bed with him? Yes. Did men like to eat food? Yes.

Once the espresso was brewing, I went over to the fridge and grabbed the bacon, eggs, and then reached into the freezer for the frozen biscuits. I was making the man breakfast. Great sex was not enough to keep him coming back. The thought made me laugh at myself. If he only knew how awkward I was, he'd rethink this. I kept my secret introverted issues undercover for the most part. I forced myself to act normal in public settings. When you have a younger sister like Phoenix that dominates a room and draws attention then soaks it up like a sponge it's hard to embrace the fact you're introverted, or you'll always be overlooked.

Mom always said I was more like her than the other two, but my mother was not introverted. She was quiet and didn't demand attention like Phoenix or fascinate people like Nate, but she had a certain beauty about her and not just her appearance. There was this inward beauty that lit up a place when she was there. Without words or actions, she became the focal point. I was not like my mother. My thoughts were not beautiful. Unlike my mother, I could be a selfish bitch.

I went to work heating up a pan to fry the bacon. While that was getting hot, I put the "made from scratch" frozen biscuits I'd bought from the grocery store on a cast iron skillet then stuck them in the oven. A complete cheat but they looked legit when they were done. I thought they tasted as good as Bliss's home-made biscuits.

My coffee was ready, so I paused to pour a cup then turned back around to find Eli standing in the living area with nothing but those athletic shorts on. His long hair was messy and the artwork on his chest and arm was literally breathtaking. The way he looked would make any woman strip naked and beg him to fuck her. See . . . bad thoughts. So not like my momma.

"Bacon," he said in a deep voice raspy from sleep. "My favorite smell to wake up to."

My cheeks were heated. I knew it. But he was standing there with his bare chest and sexy hair making my body tingle. "I hope I didn't wake you. I was trying to be quiet," I said and grabbed the eggs to start cracking in a bowl. Anything other than looking at him like he was my breakfast. I needed to get control of my flushed face too. That was embarrassing.

"You didn't. But if you had it would have been okay," he replied and although I was studying the bowl and eggs like they were a science experiment, I could see him moving closer to the kitchen. Luckily his man smell would be covered by the bacon so my hormones wouldn't go any more crazy. The sight of him was enough.

"I have to be downstairs by eight-thirty and I wanted to make sure you had breakfast, so I got started early," I was rambling, but I continued. "We had a small break after the May recital, but the toddler summer camp classes are on Saturdays in June."

He didn't respond but walked around the counter and I glanced over to see him stop in front of the espresso machine and coffee pot. He met my gaze and raised his eyebrows as if confused. "Does this side make the coffee?" he asked.

I put the eggshell down on the paper towel then quickly washed my hands before going to help him. "This already has coffee made in it," I explained, taking a mug out of the cabinet in front of him. "The other just makes espresso shots. Do you want a shot to go in your coffee?" I asked and was proud of the fact my cheeks weren't pink anymore and I appeared relaxed.

"Uh, sure," he said not sounding sure at all.

I moved at a normal pace while going through the steps to make the espresso so he could see what I was doing. Instead of the rushed way I typically did it when trying to get the caffeine quickly.

"You want me to check on the bacon?" he asked then and I realized I'd forgotten about it. Before I could reply, he was moving over to the stove and flipping the bacon. The popping sound of the grease should have been a clear enough reminder I was cooking it, but I'd been so wrapped up in Eli, I'd managed to block it all out.

"Bacon isn't on my list of things I cook well," I admitted.

He glanced back over his shoulder at me and the smile on his face said he was clearly amused by that admission. I laughed. At myself and the fact I was a terrible host. If the way to a man's heart was through his stomach, I was screwed.

Eli turned back to the bacon, but the corners of his mouth were still lifted. I liked knowing I'd put that smile there. "I'll handle the bacon. You do the eggs," he said.

I made his coffee with the shot of espresso in it then set it beside him. "Do you need sugar or cream?" I asked.

"Black is just fine," he replied and took a sip. "Damn, that'll wake you up."

I nodded as I finished with the bowl of eggs. "That's the idea."

Taking out a larger skillet for the eggs, we began cooking in silence beside each other. It wasn't weird or uncomfortable at all. This was one of the things I liked about Eli. You didn't feel like you had to speak just to fill the silence.

I wanted to stop cooking and just go sit on the sofa and watch him fry bacon with his shirt off in my kitchen. I was pretty sure that was the equivalent of porn for women.

"Fuck," he muttered and stepped back. I was jerked out of my thoughts as he stood back at arm's length while moving the bacon from the stove.

"What's wrong?" I asked, trying to figure out what had happened.

"Grease," he said simply then went to the sink to wet a paper towel. "Frying bacon without a shirt wasn't the smartest idea," he told me then he smirked as he wiped at his impressive abs. I could see the red welt the hot grease had caused.

"I'm sorry I didn't think about that," I admitted.

He lifted his amused gaze. "I don't reckon you've ever fried bacon topless before. So why would you?"

That made me laugh. He was right. I'd never fried bacon topless. Nor had a man ever done so in my presence. "Good point. Do you want me to get you some ointment?" I asked, still smiling even though he was hurt.

He shook his head. "No, it hurt but I'm not that big of a baby. It's fine." He tossed the paper towel in the trashcan then began taking the bacon out of the grease and laying it on the plate covered in paper towels I'd prepared for it.

The timer on the oven went off and I was glad I'd set it because the biscuits would have been forgotten. Cooking wasn't my strong suit and doing things in the morning that took any thought was also not my strong suit. I was struggling all the way around with this endeavor.

Grabbing an oven mitt, I got the biscuits out and set them on the marble counter. The eggs were finished and luckily I'd at least remembered to cut the burner off before walking away from them. In my rare moment of focus, I spun around to get plates only to have two large hands firmly grab my waist. I stilled instantly and all other thought slipped my mind.

Eli was standing in front of me. His head tilted so he was looking down at me. The humor from just a moment ago was gone from his expression. He stood there holding me. His fingers flexed and dug into my skin but not painfully so. Just enough to feel good.

Without saying a word, he lowered his mouth to mine and I was instantly thankful for brushing my teeth, but then I forgot even that. His kiss deepened and he held me close as we stood there tasting each other. I was lost in a moment of complete contentment.

The kiss wasn't long and ended before I was ready. Eli let his hands fall away as he stepped back. "Thanks for breakfast," he said then grinned before reaching past me and taking the plates I had been about to get. "And the kiss."

Chapter Sixteen

~ELI HARDY~

JUNE 10 / 11:34 AM

GRAN'S CHEMO TREATMENTS had started two days ago. When my dad had called to remind me, I'd been trying to decide my next move with Ophelia. We had cooked breakfast together, I'd then kissed her because I needed to touch her so damn bad. However, I'd had to end it before I took her up against the fridge like a mad man. While we ate, she told me about everything from what she had to do at work that day to her sister's current situation. I could have listened to her talk all day and been happy. She had appeared nervous at first, but as she talked, she relaxed. I asked questions and listened. That seemed to make her more comfortable too.

I had cleaned up the kitchen while she went to get ready for work. It had given me something to do and kept me busy while she was getting a shower. Knowing she had been naked in there had been hard to ignore. I didn't want her to think I was there just for the sex. The sex was amazing, but it wasn't what I needed the most. Just being near her was the one thing I couldn't seem to walk away from. I needed her.

I wouldn't have been able to leave her if it wasn't for the fact I needed to go see my gran. When I was near her, my void was forgotten. Almost as if it wasn't there. Ophelia masked it somehow. I craved that feeling of freedom her presence gave me. With her, even the silence was safe. There were no demons waiting to haunt me. She managed to keep it all away.

My uncle Preston had picked me up before noon and I'd been back in Sea Breeze by the time Gran's treatment was over. My parents, sisters, Aunt Amanda, Uncle Preston, their boys, Larissa, Micah and Jilly had already arrived at Gran's with dinner and had been sitting around the living room. The younger ones had been out at the pool. I had worried that everyone there would be too much on Gran after her treatment, but she had insisted on being put in her recliner in the living room. Even pale and weak looking she was smiling as she sat tucked under several blankets. My grandfather was the only one who was unable to act normal. The fear, worry, and concern etched on his face was clear. He had appeared to be in more pain than Gran.

My dad and Aunt Amanda were taking turns with staying there to help him with Gran through the weekend. I'd told both of them I'd stay the Monday and Tuesday then Larissa had wanted to be with her Wednesday and Thursday while she was off work. Aunt Amanda was taking Friday and half of Saturday and my dad the other half of the weekend.

Until Gran was stable and in better health, I knew I was going to be in Sea Breeze. We didn't know how long we had with her or if the chemo would give her the time we hoped it would. Leaving was not an option I could consider now.

Finding somewhere to rent short term was my first objective

on Wednesday, then I needed a job. After I got that handled, I'd need to go back to Atlanta and pick up my last paycheck at the club I had been a bouncer at for the past eight months. Then get my things from Grate's apartment. The lease on my place had been up at the end of May. I'd known when I came back here I wasn't sure where I would go next but that I wouldn't return to Atlanta to live. Grate had taken my things for me until I knew more about Gran and my plans.

That was going to take the rest of the week and weekend. Which bothered me. The only thing I wanted to do was go back to Rosemary Beach and be with Ophelia. Although she understood why I had needed to leave, it didn't ease my ache to be near her. We were keeping in contact daily through text messages and calls. I was trying to remember that getting in too deep with her was only going to end badly. But every time I thought about her, every time I talked to her, I couldn't seem to care. Feeling guilty about how she made me forget, she made me smile, it too was getting easier. If I didn't dwell on it too much.

"Eli, get yourself some sweet tea and come sit with me," Gran called from the sunroom she'd been napping in. When I had arrived this morning, my grandfather had gone to work and Gran had wanted me to bring her into the sunroom where she was going to read a book Amanda had brought her. I had gone in there to join her with a book of my own I'd taken from the study, but reading had soon put her to sleep.

I already had a glass of sweet tea, so I picked it up from the small table beside me. Afraid I'd get a call and disturb Gran's sleep, I had moved to the living room. Far enough away not to bother her rest but close enough she could call to me.

I stopped by the kitchen and took the cup of ice water that came with a lid and a straw with me too. Gran would be thirsty. I had taken her cup when I left her earlier so I could get her fresh water for when she woke up.

The sunroom was just off to the right of the kitchen. Gran had always loved this room. She kept her flowers and plants in here. When we were younger, all the girls had tea parties with Gran at the round glass table that sat in the right corner. The windows overlooked the backyard and the pool. There were memories of our childhood attached to this space. Birthday parties we'd had, summers in the pool, Easter Egg Hunts in the backyard. I knew those were also reasons Gran loved this room.

"Here's your water," I told her as I set the drink beside her. "Are you feeling hungry yet?" Her appetite was nonexistent. She was trying though. If only to keep my dad and Aunt Amanda from worrying so much.

"I'll eat in a bit. Sit and talk to me. Tell me about your time away, the people you met, and the dark shadows of pain in your beautiful eyes."

I paused for a brief second then sat down in the chair beside the recliner my grandfather had bought her recently to keep in the sunroom. If my parents had noticed, neither had mentioned it, but Gran had never been one to mince words. She got to the point. With her weakened state telling her what I'd not shared with anyone seemed like a bad idea. She'd worry about me. She needed to focus on her body and mind.

"Life outside Sea Breeze is different. I've seen a lot," I said, hoping it was enough and knowing that it wouldn't be. Not for my gran.

She cleared her throat weakly and took a drink of her water then shift slightly in her large pale blue recliner so she could see me better. The "don't bullshit me boy" frown on her face was still as intimidating as it had been in my childhood. I hadn't expected that frown and seeing something so familiar from the healthy full of life Gran I'd always known gave me hope. For her. Not me.

"I've lived my own pain right here in this town and survived. Don't tell me about having seen a lot. That's not what I'm getting at and you know it. There are scars in that soul and I can see it clearly in those eyes of yours. You can't hide that behind tattoos and a lot of hair. Not to me, you can't. It don't fool me at all." She took a deep breath and I didn't like seeing her get worked up.

I leaned forward and took her frail hand in mine. "I'm fine. Good. You need to focus on you. We all need you and I won't be fine if you don't fight through this. You need your strength and your focus needs to be on you." That was as close to honesty as Gran needed.

She sighed and then rolled her eyes at me. The reaction looked so much like my aunt Amanda, I wanted to laugh. Gran appeared younger in that moment. I wanted to remember it for the day I would need her memories to hold onto.

"You, my beautiful boy, have always had my heart. I don't do favorites, but you are your father. In looks and personality. You have his smile, his laugh, his beautiful heart. My other grandsons are their father." She shook her head in exasperation, but the soft smile on her lips made it clear my cousins were loved as dearly as I was. "I love those wild boys with a fierceness. But you get a special place because when you were born, it was like watching my Marcus grow all over again. And I see the difference deep inside you. You've been hurt in a way that will forever mark you. Now, tell your gran what happened."

I knew no matter what I did to persuade her that I was okay, she'd keep on pushing. Nothing would stop her from hitting me with questions. They'd get more direct and she'd pull all she could from me. It would be her will against mine.

I decided to give her some. Maybe it would be enough. I just couldn't give her all of it. Speaking the truth aloud was more than I could do. Even now.

"I fell in love and she was killed in a car accident." That was as truthful as I could be with Gran. The details, the other . . . I couldn't.

Gran thought about that for a few moments and I said nothing. Waiting to see what else she'd want to know. Or if she'd push for more. Finally after she stared over my shoulder with a thoughtful expression, her gaze met mine again. "What was her name?" she asked me.

"Alice," I replied, and her face was there in my memory. Not the bright beaming smile that had first drawn me in but the face . . . the face I'd had to identify . . . the face of death. Something no man is prepared for. "O'Connor," I added her maiden name just to distract myself. The memories I wanted to forget were forcing themselves to replay in my head.

"Irish," Gran pointed out.

I nodded. "Yes, both her parents moved to the states from Ireland when they were just kids." A story I'd heard about when I'd met them. The day we went to tell them we had gotten married.

"You loved her more than you'd always loved Bliss then?" she asked me. I was positive that no one else had the guts to ask me something that blunt.

I nodded. "Yeah, I did." When I'd fallen in love with Alice it had been fast, hard, exciting. Everything I'd never experienced before.

"Death is never easy. Especially for someone so young," she said. "She was loved by you though and that was a gift that I know for a fact gave her joy."

The numbness came then. It always did. I'd realized it was the way my mind handled the rest. The details that all fell into place after . . . it was over. I couldn't agree with Gran because although Alice had given me joy. Nothing had been real.

"My greatest fear is I'll always love her," I admitted without even thinking about it.

"That's not something to fear, Eli. That's something to accept. But your heart can always love her and the time you had with her and still one day love another. Just as strong. Just as hard."

Gran was never wrong. Until now. Giving someone the power to destroy me the way Alice had would always be an impossibility. That was how she'd ruined me.

Chapter Seventeen

♥ OPHELIA FINLAY ♥

JUNE 12 / 8:30 AM

I MAY HAVE gotten to sleep later this morning since Wednesday there were no dance classes in the summer, but it still took me awhile to adjust to doing things. I was on my second cup of coffee and thinking about going to the Club to get those red velvet waffles with cream cheese they had added to the breakfast menu last month. I was sure those waffles were well over a thousand calories, but I was in the mood to do something that made me smile. Eating was always one of those things.

The fact I was sulking made me pathetic. I shouldn't be sulking. Eli had a lot to do and he'd been staying with his grandmother the past two days. Of course, his first objective should be to get a place to live. Not come running here to see me. That would be ridiculous. We weren't madly in love or anything.

My mood went a little further south at that thought. I should be worried about myself. I was getting in too deep with him emotionally and it was all one-sided. That was bad. Very bad. It was never smart to be the one who cared the most. Especially with men.

I slung back the rest of my coffee before it got cold and stood up. I was going to get the damn waffles. I would then put on my bikini and go out on the sandy white beach to soak up the sun. Forget all this silliness with liking Eli too much. I was overthinking it.

The doorbell ringing confused me a moment. I stood there with my empty cup in hand frowning at the window before walking over to it. The way the instant giddiness came over me, my face burst into a grin and I ran to pick up my phone so I could open the app and tell Eli I would be right down should be more cause for concern. Instead I was too happy to give it more than a mini thought.

"That's not a face I was expecting," I said as my app opened, and his face came into view from the camera on the doorbell that was connected to it.

"You were expecting another face then?" he asked, not sounding like he was thrilled with that.

"Possibly, depends on what is in that paper bag in your hand," I teased.

He held it up and gave a small shrug. "Guess you have to take a gamble on it."

"Is it food?" I asked.

He gave a nod.

"I'll be right there!"

I heard him chuckle before I clicked off the app. That made me pause. Had I heard him laugh before? It was always a smile but not a laugh. The warmth that came from knowing I'd just made him chuckle sent me hurrying down the stairs to get to him. I slowed my pace when I was through the door in the studio where he could see me. I walked normally then, but my thoughts were only on the fact he was here to see me, and he had laughed.

I wanted to squeal and do a happy dance, but I didn't. I took a deep breath before unlocking the door to let him inside. His gaze traveled down my body and ended at my socks. With the raise of his eyebrows, I followed his gaze to my feet to see what was so interesting.

I'd forgotten I was wearing my fluffy yellow and pink pineapple socks. The oversized sweatshirt and boxers I'd slept in, he had seen before. But the socks were new. They were also bright and obnoxious if you looked at them too long. What mattered was they were soft and warm. I loved cozy socks.

"My feet were cold," I explained.

He lifted his gaze back to meet mine and gave me a very serious expression as he nodded. "Yes, I imagine with the temperature being a frigid eighty-three degrees already this morning, you are freezing."

Rolling my eyes, I stepped back and motioned for him to come inside. "I put the A/C on sixty-eight last night. I woke up and it was cold in the loft."

"Yes, I can see where sixty-eight degrees would freeze anyone's feet. Good thing you had socks made for such intense temps."

He was enjoying this a little too much. I shot him an unamused scowl then locked the door back behind him. The whole while wanting to grin like a girl with a crush. "If you weren't carrying food in your hand, I might not have let you in here. Tread carefully, Hardy." Who was I kidding? I'd have not only let him in here empty handed, I'd have also run just as quickly for the door. Sure, I loved food and I was starving, but Eli was the real treat. It was as if he knew I was sulking and came to fix it.

"It's a good thing I brought pastries from Yummy's then," he said as he held the bag up but closer to his chest as if to taunt me.

Yummy's was a famous bakery on 30A. I wasn't sure if he

knew that or if it was just a good guess. "Give me the bag," I said then added, "Please," to my demand.

He cocked his head to the side and held it even higher up and away from me. "What? I'm still getting attitude? I suggest you get sweet real fast since I have your favorites in this bag."

My favorite things at Yummy's were the cream cheese cinnamon croissants and the dark chocolate and raspberry filled cannolis. There was no way he'd know that. Yummy's was popular and had been on Food TV several times. It was easy to guess a donut lover would like Yummy's. His stopping there was a no-brainer. I would like anything he brought me. But claiming to have my favorite. . . . That was a bit of a stretch.

I placed a hand on my hip and shot him a challenging look. "Fine. If you have my favorites in that bag, then I'll share with you. If you don't then I will eat it all. To make up for the fact it's not my favorite, of course."

Eli grinned then as if he'd already won. "I need a better challenge than that. I already ate my breakfast on the way here. Smelled too good and I'd been up since five to get here this early," he replied then leaned an inch closer to my face. "If I have your favorites in this bag then you have to go with me to Sea Breeze and help me find a temporary apartment or condo. And of course you get to eat all of this by yourself. I could use some coffee though with an extra couple shots."

That was an easy gamble since that was exactly what I wanted to do. Be with him. Doing whatever he had to do. Yesterday I'd been hoping he would ask me to go with him today. When he hadn't mentioned it, I had been bummed. If he didn't have my favorites and there was a good chance he did not have my legit favorites in that bag, then I was going to go anyway.

"Deal," I said suddenly hoping he had the right things in the bag and it had nothing to do with my desire to eat.

He lowered the bag and handed it to me. I took it and now that I had it, I wasn't sure I wanted to look inside. If this wasn't my favorite items, then I would have to tell him I would still go without appearing too clingy. I could always lie about it and say whatever he bought was my favorite, but I sucked at lying. My facial expressions always gave me away.

I held his gaze as I slowly unrolled the top of the bag. The smell of cinnamon was promising as I opened it and I was mentally preparing myself not to appear disappointed when I looked inside.

Taking my eyes off his, I lowered them to the open bag and realized I'd need to take one out and see since it was wrapped in the pink wax paper I'd forgotten they used for to-go orders. When I pulled out the first round item, my heart was actually racing. I was nervous over a bakery item.

I unwrapped it and picked up the cannoli to look at the end although I could already tell it was correct. The dark chocolate was easy to see, and I smelled the familiar raspberry chocolate scent. I knew my mouth had widened into a huge grin, but this was either an excellent guess since they made seven different types of cannolis, he was a mind reader, or someone had given him this information. I lifted my head to meet his knowing smirk.

"That's a very good guess," I pointed out.

He shrugged as if it was no big deal.

"I have more than one favorite though," I added just to be difficult. Now that I knew he had somehow found out my favorites. This was fun.

"Really? Well, why don't you check that bag more thoroughly," he drawled.

I rolled my cannoli up and put it back in the bag then moved a second cannoli out of the way to find a larger item wrapped on the bottom. Taking it out I couldn't see it, but I knew. I just knew. It was the correct size and as I unwrapped it, the sweet cinnamon smell rose to meet my nose. I laughed as the paper fell away and the correct croissant was in my hand. This time when I looked up at him his former smirk was a victorious smile.

"Okay, you cheated. Yummy's has too many things for you to nail this spot on." I paused then added, "Not that I won't agree to your terms of the challenge. I just need to know how you pulled this off."

I was getting to spend my day with him, and I was thrilled. Protecting my emotions were apparently shot to hell since I reacted like this to the man. How had he gotten to me so easily? I was normally more careful. Eli was becoming more and more of an addiction. I lit up when I saw his name on my phone. Even the text messages I got from him made me smile.

"I'm all knowing," he replied, and his eyes held laughter. It was so rare to see that in those green pools that my heart warmed. He was lying of course, but he was happy. I was making him happy. The darkness that he carried with him was showing up less and less when we were together, and every little breakthrough made me let down my own walls even more.

Oh, who was I kidding? I had no walls where he was concerned. I'd already accepted it. I needed to stop thinking I had any willpower left against Eli.

"You, sir, are withholding the truth. But I want to eat, so let's go upstairs," I said then spun around and started toward the stairs. The smell of the food and the joy I was currently feeling made me hungry. I reached inside and pulled a cannoli from the paper wrap then took a bite.

"Mmmm, God these are like heaven," I moaned as I chewed it slowly.

When we reached the loft, I had left the door open in my quick escape to go let him inside as if I didn't he would disappear. Walking in without having to open the door was good since I had a bag in one hand and a cannoli in the other. I had to tilt my head back and catch some of the chocolatey goodness trying to fall out of the end I hadn't taken a bite from.

Closing my eyes, I savored it and then licked what I had missed from my lips. Once I was finished, I set the bag down on the kitchen counter and turned to see Eli watching me closely. His eyes were darker now but not in a bad way. More of an . . . excited way.

"You keep eating like that and I'm going to have you naked and pushed back on the bar stool with your legs straddling me."

His words made every nerve in my body come alive that weren't already slightly humming at the sight of him. I inhaled deeply and the beating of my heart was in my ears. I would gladly strip my clothing off for him and sit down on this stool if he asked. My stomach was no longer important, but the sensitive area between my thighs had now started to ache in a deliciously painful way.

"Oh." I may have sighed as I said it. I was out of breath and we hadn't done anything. I'd taken several baths with a toy the past few days thinking about the first and only time Eli and I had come together.

I had wished more than once that he'd climbed on top of me Friday night or Saturday morning. Or sometime in between. My entire body began to tingle when I thought of how good he felt. He was larger than any of my past sexual experiences and I now got why girls liked them bigger. I had always thought it would be uncomfortable, but it wasn't. Not at all.

"Eat." His words sounded like an order. Right now, the idea of him ordering me around was exciting. I opened the bag and took the second cannoli out. Before I took a bite, he walked past me toward the espresso machine.

He wasn't going to fuck me and I was aching for it. Damn. I had to get control of myself. When had I started thinking about sex all the time? Oh, that's right. When Eli had shown me how amazing it could be.

"I called Bliss last night when I decided to come bribe you into spending the day with me condo hunting. She asked Nate and he called your mom who knew exactly what would work," he was explaining the food as if I cared. I was past that.

I chose to eat instead of try and speak.

He managed to fix the coffee correctly and get the espresso shots going as well. When he had accomplished both, he turned around to look at me. "Have you eaten it all?" he asked.

I had eaten half of the second cannoli and decided to put it down and eat the croissant before I got too full to enjoy it. I'd only managed to get half of it eaten. Possibly because I wasn't hungry for food anymore.

"I can't eat it all. I tried," I explained. The two half-eaten items were on the bakery paper in front of me.

Eli walked over to it and picked up the cannoli. "Can I try it?" he asked before taking a bite.

"Of course," I told him then added, "but don't blame me for your instant addiction." I was trying to lighten the mood. My mood that is. He seemed fine. The sexual threat in his eyes was now gone. That quickly.

"It's good. But the caramel cream cheese one I had on the way here was better," he countered with a gleam in his eyes expecting me to argue.

"I've never tried the caramel so I can't be sure that you are wrong. But I am going to go with my gut that dark chocolate and raspberry will always beat anything caramel."

Eli finished it off then shook his head. "We will just agree to disagree. Caramel is always better." Then he added, "To me at least."

I would remember that for the future. My mom could make

the world's best caramel cake. It had been her mother's recipe. I wasn't sure I could pull it off without Mom's guidance or her just doing it while I watched, but I was getting him one.

The coffee finished and he turned to begin fixing his drink. "Do you want me to make you one? Or do you trust me to get it right?" he asked as he pulled down a cup like he had been here a million times. I liked how comfortable he seemed. In the past, a man feeling comfortable in my home always bothered me. Made me feel suffocated. This was one more thing that I realized was different. Everything I felt for Eli was different.

"I've had my caffeine for the morning but thank you," I told him.

When he turned back to me with his cup in hand, he gave me that grin I was seeing more and more of. The one I hoped he didn't give to anyone else. "Then you better go get dressed. We have a drive ahead of us and a full day. That is if you're still planning on holding up your end of the bargain."

HA! As if I would let him leave without me. The uncertainty I saw for just a second in his gaze made me feel a little relief that he wasn't aware just how sunk I was. No man needed that power. Not this soon.

Chapter Eighteen

~ELI HARDY~

JUNE 12 / 4:46 PM

FINDING A FURNISHED place that I could rent monthly without a long-term lease had been more difficult than I'd hoped. However, Krit Corbin had called me two hours ago to tell me that the condo he owned was currently empty. My mom had given him a call when she found out I was looking for somewhere to live. I hadn't thought to ask him about it. I figured he had it rented out weekly for the summer. It had once been an apartment complex when he had lived there before marriage and kids. However, as Sea Breeze built up and the tourism began to grow, it had turned into primarily vacation rentals. Which meant the place was fully furnished and I needed nothing but my clothing.

I was relieved when we went to meet Krit there and look at it. Not that I thought I wasn't going to find a place. We had seen two places that might have worked for me. I had been waiting on a callback from both. I had been relieved because it wasn't even four yet and that meant I got to spend time with Ophelia doing something other than this.

Although she had appeared to be having fun today. She made it enjoyable. Just watching her and listening to her talk. She was extra chatty after she drank some cold girlie coffee drink around noon. I'd liked seeing her that way. I liked seeing her every way if I was completely honest.

I hadn't worried about getting my clothes from Gran's yet. I would deal with that when Ophelia was back in Rosemary Beach. I didn't want to bring up the drive back there just yet. She was checking out the items in the kitchen cabinet currently and telling me different things I may need. I listened but only because I liked hearing her talk. For someone who didn't cook a lot, she had several opinions on kitchen necessities.

"The fact the beach is right out there makes me envious. That's the one thing I miss. Growing up having the view of the gulf from my bedroom window spoiled me, I guess. I think I don't need it until I see how calming it is. When I do buy my own place, it'll be on the water."

The image of her buying a house on the beach came along with an unknown man who she would marry. My mood turned sour. That wasn't something I wanted to think about. I shook it off and decided we needed to do something less domestic.

"Are you hungry? That sandwich earlier wasn't much. I think I'm ready for something more." I knew my sudden change in subject had thrown her off, but she didn't question it.

"Sure. This is your town. What's good?" she asked.

I was about to suggest Live Bay but thought of the people we would most likely see there and sharing her didn't sound appealing. I'd avoided as many family and friends as I could so far. I knew they would ask questions I wasn't going to answer. I also didn't like the idea of those memories the questions would resurface affecting my time with Ophelia.

She was my escape from the hollowness. I wanted to keep it that way.

I watched as she walked around the island in the kitchen then toward me. She didn't say anything because she was waiting on my suggestion. The sway of her hips always drew my gaze to her body. She had a way of walking that was hard to ignore. Even if her face wasn't so damn gorgeous it would stop traffic, the way she carried her body would be equally dangerous.

I forgot what it was I had been supposed to say as I watched her come to a stop a few inches from me. The frayed blue jean skirt she had on today was short enough that I'd had a hard time not staring at her instead of looking at the different places we'd checked out.

I tore my eyes off her tanned legs before I could start fantasizing over slipping my hand between her legs and running it up until I could touch the warmth at the top. As I lifted my gaze, her hard nipples pressing against the soft snug fitting cotton of her tank top made my already stiffening cock grow. Fuck.

I'd been so good this morning. When I'd seen her, all I could think of was fucking her in every room of the loft. Until we both passed out sweaty and sated. As much as I wanted to feel her, touch every inch of her and be inside her, I also feared not being able to walk away when the time came. I knew how unforgettable sex with her was.

Then there was the complete opposite fear that our night together had been because of the wine she'd drunk. What if the explosive chemistry wasn't the same? My body seemed to think it would be. I was so damn tense as I fought the desire to reach out and grab her.

"Eli," she said my name in a low sultry tone that caused me to jerk in reaction. I tore my eyes off her breast and met her gaze. The blue of her eyes had darkened, and her bottom lip was swollen as if she'd been biting it. I stared at her and let all the uncertainty fade away.

"Take off your top." I knew it sounded like a command as my voice had gone gravelly with the need taking over me.

She inhaled sharply. There was pure excitement blazing in her eyes. She reached down and took the hem of her top then slowly pulled it up her body. It was like a fucking striptease. Each inch that she eased up, I held my breath. All damn day I'd seen her breasts bounce under that top. The thin satin fabric of her bra barely contained them.

Both of my hands were fisted against my thighs when she finally pulled the top over her head and tossed it away.

"The bra," I growled. Hoping it was just as painfully slow but equally wanting it to be quick.

She continued in her patient movements. There was no ripping off of clothing and as much as the wait excited me, the more I wanted to reach out and do it myself. By the time she was fiddling with the back clasp of her bra, my hands were so tightly fisted my very short nails were somehow managing to dig into my skin.

Ophelia held her hands over each satin cupped breast for just a moment, but it felt as if it were an eternity. Our gazes held, transfixed, her desire just as strong as mine. It was shining in her eyes and I moved then, ready to rip the damn bra off when she let her hands fall and the bra slid off her arms and down to drop at the floor. Both beautiful breasts were revealed, and I was stuck taking in the sight of her smooth perfect skin.

Instead of asking her to continue the striptease I knew I couldn't handle any more. I had to touch her, taste her, smell her. My hands gripped her waist as I closed the distance between us. Holding her tightly against me I wished I had taken my shirt off too. Just so the warmth of my chest could feel her with nothing between us.

For now, I lowered my mouth to capture hers and forget everything else but the connection. How her taste became all I remembered, all I cared about. Nothing painful could touch me when Ophelia was in my arms. It was everything I'd never known or expected.

Her soft purrs of pleasure as her hands lifted to my head so her fingers could thread through my hair gave my pulse even more of a jolt. I began to leave a trail of soft kisses on her neck and then down slowly toward her shoulder. Taking a soft bite on the tender skin at the base of her neck, I breathed deeply at her reaction. Both of her hands fisted tightly in my hair and her body arched toward me. Unable to wait any longer, I found her left breast and kissed it before pressing my tongue on the pebbled nipple then drawing it into my mouth to suck.

"AH!" she cried out and her hands stopped running through my hair but instead held my head to her breast. I bit down gently, and she made more sounds as her body pressed closer to my mouth. While I kissed and enjoyed every sound she made, my throbbing with the need to be inside her grew stronger.

I moved my head to the right breast and gave it equal attention, but my hands moved to the buttons on her skirt. Easily enough I managed to get it unfastened and slipping to the floor at her feet. Her hands left my head then and she was pulling on the bottom of my shirt. Reluctantly letting her nipple free of my mouth, I straightened and allowed her to pull my shirt off before letting my gaze take in the sight of her standing there in only her panties.

This kitchen would never be the same. I'd see her every time I walked in here. Looking like every fantasy I'd ever had. She'd mark this place with her presence, and I wanted her to. She made life better.

Her hands were on the snap and zipper of my jeans. I took over then needing this as equally if not more so than she did. My jeans were undone, and I pushed them down then stepped out of them and shoved them aside. The black boxer briefs I was wearing and her pink lace panties were all that stood between us now.

Grabbing the sides of her head, I kissed her again. This time with the hunger, craving, and desperate want that was hammering through me. Demanding I take more. Wanting to experience her again. To be taken to that delirious crazed release that only she brought me.

Her hands grabbed my waist and then a moment later they slipped inside my briefs. I stopped breathing when her hand slid down and took my rigid cock in her grasp. With one soft pump of her hand, I cracked. I couldn't prolong this anymore. I tore my mouth off hers and reached for her panties. In my haste to free her, I ripped the tiny straps on each side and tossed them away not willing to wait until she slid them down her legs.

The surprise in her eyes wasn't fear and hopefully wasn't anger at my destroying her lace under thing, but I had to be inside her. I grabbed her waist and put her on the stool beside me. Her thighs opened and her knees lifted as if we had choreographed this. I shoved my briefs down far enough to be free then took her legs and pushing them farther apart before slamming into her body.

The tightness clenched me, yet I slid in easily with her body ready to take me.

"OH GOD!" she yelled, and her head fell back. Her eyes were closed, breasts jutting out and not one fucking goddess I'd ever seen depicted looked close to as beautiful as Ophelia in this moment.

I trembled at the sight of her. Being deep inside her made all the wrongs in my life disappear. I held her waist again and my mouth went to her exposed neck to lick and kiss while I started rocking my hips and slowly pulling back then sliding in hard so that both of us were given the deepest sensation.

"Eli," she breathed my name grabbing my head and holding my face close to her neck. My breath hot against her skin, the scent that was uniquely Ophelia surrounding me, engulfing me. "Harder, I need you harder," she panted.

"Fuck," I growled as the man who was trying to give her pleasure began to morph into a hungry animal at her request. I wanted to pound into her until we were both screaming our release. As heavenly as she felt with each slide into her body, I knew the moment I began slamming inside her it would lead to earth-shattering release.

"Please," she begged when I didn't immediately begin fucking her the way she wanted. The desperation in her plea sent me barreling into the darkness, intent on giving her what she wanted and what I craved.

My hands moved to grab her ass and the soft flesh filled my hands. "You want to be fucked hard, baby?" I asked as I gave her the first forceful entry.

"YES!" she cried as our bodies slapped against each other.

Squeezing the plumpness in my hands, I let the monster clawing inside me free and hammered her willing body.

"OH GOD! YES! AHHHH!" Her cries drove me on. The attempt to allow her to savor it was gone. Desire, need, and pleasure were leading us both.

"So fucking wet," I said into her ear. "You're soaked. Naughty girl gets hot over being fucked hard." I was triggering her, and I knew it. She wanted to hear the words.

Her body shook and her nails clawed at my back. "Yes," she panted. "I want it," she agreed. My words were sending her closer to a release.

"This sweet tight pussy is mine. It wants me to fuck it. I want to lay you down and taste it. Lick you until you can't take anymore."

"OH GOD!" she moaned, and her head fell back again just as her body began to shake and I could feel the first clench of her orgasm on my dick. "ELI! OH!" she managed to choke out. I kept going. This wasn't it. I would make sure she had more than one. Even if the pull to follow right behind her to my own release was strong. If I could hold off long enough, I'd give her three.

"You want my tongue sliding inside you?" I whispered close to her ear then bit the lobe. "Flicking your clit until it hurts you want to come so bad? Giving me all that sweetness on my tongue. Then I'll pump you with my dick again until I'm coming so deep inside you we are both fucking lost."

I was exciting myself with the image I was describing to her. The sounds she was making told me it was doing the same for her. The frenzy building in her again soared and with a loud cry, the next orgasm hit her. She bucked wildly beneath me. My name coming from her lips in gasps. Watching her, hearing her begging me to stop, to keep going, it all drove me harder. She didn't know what she was saying and it no longer mattered. The roaring in my ears muffled everything and I gripped her hips, she lifted her knees as if I'd asked her to. Her eyes opened and she watched me pumping into her. Her breathing hard, breasts bouncing, when she licked her lips I broke.

The climax was an explosion. The kind of euphoria that claimed you.

"FUCK!! HOLY. . . . GAH!" I yelled the words as the most intense moment of my life rocked through my body.

"ELI! I can feel it! Oh!" She once again began to quake and the third orgasm I wanted to give her crashed through her body.

I pulled her against my chest. My body still experiencing tremors of pleasure.

Even if this woman found a way to destroy an already broken man, I would never regret it. Some moments were worth losing your soul over.

Chapter Nineteen

♥ OPHELIA FINLAY ♥

JUNE 12 / 10:06 PM

I LAY IN my bed watching Eli sleep. He'd held me as we fell asleep together. Or I pretended to fall asleep until he was breathing deep and even. My thoughts weren't going to allow me to shut down that easily. Today had been perfect. Too perfect.

I closed my eyes tightly and sighed as the tenderness between my legs reminded me of the thorough job of fucking my brains out Eli had done earlier. Finding him a place to live had taken up most of our day. I had been happy when he found this place but accepting the fact this was temporary and he'd leave again one day made me panic. It was what kept me awake. More than once today I had heard him tell an owner or real estate agent he wasn't looking for permanent residence. A reminder he didn't want to stay. Whatever life he'd left to return here was important to him.

My desperation to keep him had been what drove me to be

so wild when we had sex. I realized when it was over, I'd been trying to cling to him or possibly find a way to hold him. I knew that I would only hurt myself more when he left if I allowed my heart to think he might decide to stay. The safest thing for me to do was to take all I could while I had him here. It had been my goal when I'd let all my walls down. I had opened myself up emotionally and physically to Eli. Living in the now, taking all he gave me, begging for more, wanting to know the feeling of being one with Eli.

It had been mind-blowing, best I've ever had, make that the best anyone had ever had, sex. There was just no way it got better than that. There couldn't be any comparison. What we experienced together had to be the pinnacle of sex. Historically so. I didn't question it . . . because I knew that while I was giving my body to that man, he took my heart too. Sex that incredible and real coupled with the giving of your heart was on a level of unattainable that many would never know. I closed my eyes even tighter. Fear grabbed my throat so tightly I found it hard to breathe. I'd never done this. Not once had I just let a man have it. My walls had been put in place from a young love that had hurt me. One I hadn't realized at the time was just innocence getting its first taste of desire. That hadn't truly been love. Not now that I knew this feeling. The unquestionable soul claiming kind of love I'd fell straight into with Eli.

Accepting it and admitting it were one in the same. There was no way to save me now. No possible wall building could change what had transpired. I wouldn't be able to backtrack and run away. I was taken. Leaving him would be impossible. My heart wouldn't allow it. Eli Hardy owned my body and soul whether he wanted it or not. Not completely losing my head and telling him I loved him during that last orgasm when I had known it was the truth had been my only saving grace. If I'd told him I loved him, he quite possibly may not be in my bed with me right now. He didn't have to say it, I knew he wasn't after love. Not mine or anyone else's. I hadn't meant to fall. It wasn't something I could have controlled.

The reality that I was in love had shocked me. I hadn't been vulnerable enough to feel this way about a man in the past. Why Eli? Why did I fall for a man who made it clear this was as temporary as his apartment? My stone will not to break had let me down this time. I'd broken, or melted was a more accurate description.

I inhaled deeply and the smell of his soap made me feel warm all over. If I could climb into his skin and just be with him every moment, I'd be happy. That would be the ultimate joy. And admitting that to myself made me sound like a crazy ass person who should be admitted. What was wrong with me? I was thinking insane things and I had to face the fact this man was going to leave me. This wasn't a fairy tale. I wasn't going to win the man. He wasn't open to being won. He was passing the time. If I was smarter, I would have found a way to protect my heart before this had happened.

Distancing myself now was impossible. The idea took my breath away. I never wanted to be away from him again. I'd let a man become the center of my world. How? I opened my eyes and looked at him again. His long blonde lashes and straight nose. The dark blonde curls from his hair resting against his cheek. He was a man, but he was also achingly beautiful. I didn't understand how a woman could not want him forever.

Lila Kate and even my own sister-in-law seemed like fools to me now. I hadn't known Eli when both of them hadn't returned his love. My mother would say that the heart sees the one it was meant to love differently than any other. That couldn't be what was happening here because this was a one-sided love. My loving Eli didn't guarantee he'd ever feel the same for me.

Jealousy began to slowly take hold when I thought of how Lila Kate had talked about Eli's deep love for Bliss. How he'd never get over her. How he'd loved her his whole life. Was I really going to lie here and hate the woman that made my brother happy because of Eli? I was going mental. Did love make you go mental? Was it possible that Eli was the one my heart was supposed to love and that in time he'd feel the same way? My chest felt lighter at that possibility.

I had to talk to someone. I needed guidance and help understanding this and what I was feeling. It scared me. I wanted to kiss him until he woke up and we were joined again. Making love. I wanted to tell him I loved him . . . and then he'd most likely leave and never come back. That would send him running just like those words had sent me running from men in the past.

Karma . . . this could be karma. Had it finally decided I needed a swift kick in the ass? I muffled a groan in my pillow.

Crazy. I was going crazy. Or was this normal? Is this why men said women were crazy? Did love make women crazy? There was a song about it . . . "Beautiful Crazy" or something like that. Which a man had written so there was hope I could be loved back even with all this craziness I was feeling.

Eli sighed in his sleep and shifted then rolled over onto his back. He moved his arm from around me and laid it over his head to rest on the pillow. The blanket fell down enough so that now I was given the glorious view of his tattooed chest and neck. I wanted to kiss it all. Ask him about each one. Find out what they meant.

My enjoyment instantly vanished as the question hit me . . . was one of the tattoos for Bliss? The girl who had been given his heart and didn't want it? I felt sick. An all over sick. I hated that idea. I wanted to erase it from my head. Why was I torturing myself like this? There was no reason for it. I had to get a grip.

I knew who I could talk to. The person who would have the

answers. She would be able to tell me if I needed to seek professional help. The one woman I knew loved a man with every fiber of her being and had my entire life and before my birth.

My momma. She knew all about love. Finding the one your heart belongs to. Often, I saw married women unhappy or look at their husbands with distaste. I saw their eyes wander to see the grass on the other side of the fence. But never once had I seen my momma do that. When she looked at my dad, it was such a pure look of love and respect it gave me hope in happily ever after.

Their love wasn't one-sided. I wasn't sure if it had ever been. What I did know was my dad adored the ground my mother walked on and there was no equal to her. Even growing up, we knew our father loved us, he would die for us, we were his children and we never questioned his devotion. However, he also made it clear that our mother was his one. His other half. Once Phoenix had been angry at Momma and claimed to hate her. She often said hurtful things around the ages of fourteen to seventeen.

Dad had moved quickly. One minute we'd all been sitting around the kitchen table while Phoenix and Momma had a heated argument about one of the bad decisions my sister had made. Then my dad was in her face, taking her arm and standing her up from the seat. Although I wasn't scared for her because Dad had never once laid a hand on us, I was startled by his reaction. His words still rang clear in my memory.

"That woman is your mother, she carried you, gave birth to you, loved you from the moment she knew of your existence, lost sleep caring for you, and would die for you if asked. But not only that, she is mine. She is what completes me. And I won't allow ANYONE to speak to her that way. Including our children. Because without her, there would be no you. Do I make myself clear?"

Those words had sunk in deep and stayed there not only in Phoenix but all of us.

Love was defined by those words my father said to her that day. It was how I measured every relationship I'd ever had. None coming close. As thankful and blessed as I knew we were to have parents that loved like they did, in time I had told myself it was impossible to find.

Until now, I was so consumed by these feelings that had broken free inside me for Eli. Only my mother would understand. Maybe she'd be able to help me make him feel the same way. I didn't think it worked like that, but I had to hope there was a way to keep him. I pressed my lips to his arm and let my eyes close again. I didn't focus on the worries of loving a man I could lose. Instead, I thought of all the moments today that made me smile and let that happiness go with me into the peacefulness of sleep.

Chapter Twenty

~ELI HARDY~

JUNE 13 / 12:06 PM

THE SOUNDS OF little girl voices faded. I glanced up from my laptop to see it was noon. Ophelia had said she would have a two-hour break from twelve to two. I should have driven back to Sea Breeze this morning. I needed to get settled in my apartment, find a job, and decided on going back to Atlanta to get my things or just calling and seeing if Grate would ship me what I had left with him. I was almost positive the club I had worked at would mail me the paycheck they still had of mine.

I'd woken to find Ophelia curled up asleep at my side with her arms wrapped around mine as if she was trying to get close to me even in her sleep. I'd decided one more day wouldn't hurt. I didn't want to face reality when I had this here. I didn't want to go back to Atlanta now that I knew how being near Ophelia made me feel alive again.

The freedom from darkness that being with Ophelia provided,

getting to see her smile, listen to her laugh, just fucking getting to be in her presence was a cure to the emptiness. It was like the universe was telling me I'd lived through hell and she was my reward. That idea made me feel guilty. I had shoved it away. Ophelia was beauty and for a moment I was getting to experience it. She had some power to weave that beauty around everything around her.

I'd stayed this morning because of all that and unlike our sexual explosiveness from the day before, we had taken it slow in the early hours of dawn. Savored being there together. I'd kissed her and for a moment it was just us. Nothing else in the world. As life-altering as the previous sex with her had been, this morning had been spiritual. To describe it as making love wasn't adequate.

The door opened to the loft and every nerve in my body reacted to knowing she was back. Close again. Here with me. I was completely screwed, and I knew it. The idea of leaving her seemed impossible. Atlanta and all it harbored felt like a different lifetime.

I couldn't label this insanity she'd created inside me as love. I'd been in love. More than once and I knew how love felt. This was a different power altogether. One I had no name for. I wasn't sure anyone had a name for the reaction that just the thought of her released within me.

"I'm starving," she announced as she lit up the place with her smile. "Want to go with me to find food? Because cooking something doesn't sound appealing at all."

I closed my laptop and stood up. "Where do you want to go?" I asked. She had only enough time to grab a banana and a protein bar on her way out the door this morning.

Her expression was one of deep thought before she held up a finger and said with obvious excitement, "I know!"

I didn't care where it was or what kind of food they had. I was with her and it made the world a brighter place. "Let's go then," I said, grabbing my keys from the table.

"Do you like Thai food?" she asked, studying me as if she was expecting me to lie and she needed to decipher the truth.

"It's not my favorite, but I'm willing to try it," I replied honestly enough.

Then she broke out into a massive grin before laughing. "I hate Thai food," she said while still laughing. "You're in luck. Masters is a barbecue place."

I cocked an eyebrow and kept the amusement off my face. "Damn, I hate barbecue," I lied.

She laughed harder before responding, "Nice try. I've seen you eat a plate full of barbecue chicken at Nate and Bliss's engagement party. And you went back to get seconds on the fixings."

That made me pause and take it in. She had paid that close of attention to me that night she remembered what I ate? How did I process that? Was it simply because she was sizing me up back then being her brother's fiancée's best friend and a male? Or was it because she wanted to look at me?

"Don't go thinking into that so much," she said with a roll of her eyes. "I people watch."

I smirked then. If she felt the need to cover for the fact she remembered a small detail like that about me, then she'd been studying me for more than just people watching.

"Then tell me what someone else ate that night," I challenged. "If you were people watching, I couldn't have been the only one you watched."

The pink that instantly colored her cheeks said more than anything else she could say at this point. Was it possible the Eli I was before the shit I'd lived through changed me had been attractive to Ophelia? Could it be something about me other than my appearance and hardening that drew her to me?

Motherfucker. It was pulling me. That invisible string that was slowly thickening into a more solid structure. Making her more important. More required. More wanted by me than was safe. For either of us.

"Fine," she said, regaining her air of confidence she held so well. "I was watching only you. I was intrigued."

I felt like she was going to say more but didn't. I wanted to push, but I refrained. She'd admitted enough. Her flushed cheeks told me she felt vulnerable about me knowing it. I didn't want her to regret opening up to me that way.

I walked toward her and only stopped when we were an inch apart. "You were impossible not to watch. Every single man in the room was looking at you. The ribs you ate not giving one shit that your dress was white or that the sauce was on your face while you enjoyed them was fucking sexy." I had many memories of her. Admitting them all would be a mistake. But this I would give her so that she felt as if we were on equal footing.

The wide-eyed reaction I got from my admitting my memory as she stared up at me with surprise was so damn adorable, I lowered my head and kissed her. The more I gave her of myself, the more I knew I'd regret. Where Ophelia was sunlight and positivity, I was darkness and pain. This feeling she gave me couldn't last forever. My demons would eventually be stronger as I grew accustomed to her. Time would expose how unsuitable I was for someone like her.

If only the man I'd been before I left had known she was looking. Would it have made me stay? I had never regretted leaving until now. Her hands ran up my arms as she kissed me back just as passionately. If I didn't step back, she'd end up hungry still and back at work. My desire to be inside her couldn't be the only thing I focused on.

I ended the kiss, stepped back from her and nodded toward the door behind her. "We need to feed you."

She gave a soft laugh then. "Probably should get out of this loft before I forget I'm hungry."

"Lead the way," I replied in agreement, staying alone with her one more second was going to be too much. If we were going to eat, we needed to escape before the passion beating hot just under the surface broke free again.

"I have more fruit and I think some peanut butter. I could eat here," she said without moving.

That was fucking tempting. "Go, now, before I change my mind. You need more than that to eat."

I saw the indecision in her eyes.

"Sweet Jesus you're gonna kill me, GO," I said the last as a demand.

The saucy grin she flashed me before turning and walking back out the door eased the sexual tension enough to make me chuckle.

Chapter Twenty-One

♥ OPHELIA FINLAY ♥

JUNE 15 / 5:37 PM

I HAD EXPECTED the Saturday afternoon traffic to be worse than it was along the coast. My drive from Rosemary Beach to Sea Breeze had only taken two hours exactly. Once the dance camp ended today, I'd already had my bags in the car to come this way.

Eli had left to come back here Thursday after we had gone to lunch. While eating, he got a call from his dad about his grandmother not doing well after her chemo treatment that morning. Eli had felt like he should go back and check on her.

Watching him drive away had been hard, but the reason why made me love him more. He hadn't even gotten back to Sea Breeze when he texted me that he'd be back this weekend if all was well. I'd immediately told him that after work today I'd come to him.

Finding a parking spot was easy enough. Most people were probably out on a Saturday night. I reached over and took my overnight bag from the passenger seat then stepped out of the car. The sound of the beach being so close made it feel like home, even though it was a very different place. Glancing up toward Eli's apartment, the light was on and his bike was parked in his designated parking spot. He was expecting me.

I was hungry and hoped we ate soon. All I'd had at work today was microwaveable mac and cheese. Then on the other hand, if Eli wanted to strip me naked and give me a few orgasms first, I wouldn't be opposed to that either. I'd thought of little else since he'd left my place. As much as I loved the slow lovemaking we'd had last, I was in the mood for being taken roughly tonight. I liked his dirty mouth. Thinking about it excited me.

By the time I reached the stairs that led up to his apartment, I was grinning. Anticipating wild sex possibly on his kitchen table or maybe his sofa. However, the closer I got to his door the louder the voices were. When I knocked on it, I knew there was several people in there. Eli hadn't said anything about others being here when I called him earlier.

The door swung open and Eli's sister, Crimson, answered. She was striking with red hair and pale skin like her mother's. The smile that spread across her face at the sight of me was a relief. I'd never gotten to talk to Crimson much and I knew very little about her. I wanted Eli's family to like me.

"I now understand why Eli was so annoyed by our arrival," Crimson said, stepping back and opening the door wider for me to enter. "Micah brought the beer, I brought brownies and red wine, and Jude brought his momma's homemade lasagna with garlic bread. Looks like our housewarming meal was not in his plans tonight," she was explaining all this to me I realized.

I stepped into the apartment as Eli walked toward me scowling. When he reached me, he took the bag from my hand. "They just walked in," he told me and from the look on his face, I was wondering if he intended to kick them out. I hoped not. I didn't want to be the reason he kicked his family out. I knew Micah was married to Eli's Aunt Larissa. So that made him and his younger brother, Jude, family. I glanced over and saw no one else. Just these three.

"I'm starving," I said, looking at Crimson. "I'd love some of the lasagna, garlic bread, and a brownie or three."

Crimson's smile brightened and she then shot her brother a smirk. "See, she's hungry. Now go put her bag up and stop glaring at us all like we are intruders. Because we obviously are, but we did come with food and beverages."

Eli's scowl didn't fade as he walked off with my bag back toward the bedroom.

"You're Nate's sister," Micah Falco said then as if he'd been trying to place me and it just hit him.

I gave him a nod. "Guilty."

"I won't lie, we had no idea you and my brother were uh . . . close. I mean I remember you and him walking down to the beach the night he arrived at Bliss's, but I didn't know you were seeing each other . . ." Her last few words faded off as if they were more of a question. I couldn't blame Eli for not telling anyone. I hadn't told my family either. It was all kind of new. I was planning on talking to my mother about things, but I hadn't done so yet. I was almost afraid to bust the happy bubble I was currently in with Eli.

"It's the tattoos, isn't it?" Micah said, shaking his head with a chuckle. "Damn kid gets all inked and goes from nerd to player overnight."

Micah Falco had been at enough of the same events as me that I knew he was the one with all the comments and often funny yet inappropriate one-liners. He was good for diffusing awkward moments too. I had witnessed it a few times. However, I didn't like him referring to Eli as a nerd.

"The ink is hot, but Eli has been on my radar well before he disappeared. I just hadn't worked up the nerve to make a move yet." Okay so maybe that wasn't the exact truth, but it made Micah's mocking grin morph into an impressed wide-eyed expression.

"Well, damn, dude," he said as Eli walked back into the room. "I didn't realize you had such fucking game before you ran off."

"Ignore Micah, we all do," Crimson said just before there was another knock on the door.

"Motherfucker," Eli muttered, and Crimson ignored him to open it up.

"Please tell me that's spinach artichoke dip." Crimson's voice was one of longing as she moved out of the way and Bliss walked in carrying a bag of chips followed by my brother carrying a bowl I assumed was the dip Crimson was hoping for.

"Of course it is," Bliss said, grinning at her. "I couldn't show up without bringing your favorite—" She stopped mid-sentence as her gaze met mine. It went from confused to surprised.

"You invited that brat?" My brother's tone was teasing, so I shot him the annoyed snarl I always did when he called me a brat.

"I feel better about being in the dark now," Crimson said with a small laugh. It seemed Crimson had set up this surprise house warming party. My brother had been speaking to her when he'd mentioned me being invited. Crimson was realizing Nate had no idea about me and Eli either.

"The dark?" Nate asked, setting the bowl down on the bar before turning toward the rest of the room.

Eli's hand rested on my lower back at that moment and the warmth of his body felt comforting as he stepped up to my left side. Close enough that it made things very clear.

Nate's eyebrows shot up then as he took in the obvious non-verbal statement. "Really?" he asked, sounding amazed. "With her smartass mouth and attitude? You've seen that side of her, right?"

"I am not above kicking your ass in front of all these nice people," I warned Nate. Who then laughed and shook his head.

"Not even on a good day, little sister. Damn, I thought after the movie premier whatever was going on with the two of you was done." I could see in his eyes as they locked with mine that he was good with this. Amused but pleased. With Eli and Bliss's history, I hadn't been sure how he would feel. I hadn't cared, to be honest, but it was nice to see he was cool with it. Happy even.

I swung my gaze to Bliss then realizing she may not be as pleased. I knew she loved my brother fiercely and I wasn't worried about her feeling as if she had some claim on Eli. But she was my sister-in-law. Eli was her best friend. Neither of us had told her and she was walking into it blindsided. Like everyone else.

She went from studying Eli then her thoughtful gaze shifted to me. Slowly a smile began to tug at the corners of her mouth. "I wondered after the movie premier . . . and leaving Eli there but then neither of you said anything," she said as if it was all falling into place. "Good." Was all she said then and gave me a warm smile that matched the expression in her eyes. "I won't hold it against y'all for not telling me since not even your siblings knew," she added with a shrug then walked over to hand Nate the chips she was carrying.

"You're not going to warn him about her?" my brother asked Bliss.

"Hell, Finlay, she can't be worse than you and we all had to let you have our sweet innocent Bliss," Micah said as he walked over to take the cover from the dip. "Eli's all brooding and sexy now. Sure she's gorgeous, possibly out of his league but they're dating. Let's eat before anymore damn family shows up and we got to go through this all over again."

The silent Jude finally stood up from the place on the sofa

he'd been sitting quietly. "Thank God, I'm starving to death while this fucking live action soap opera unravels."

I turned my head to look up at Eli. He wasn't scowling as bad, but he still didn't appear thrilled about this. "They did bring food," I whispered.

He met my gaze then. "Crimson should have asked me first," he said.

"Saved us from having to tell them," I added another pro to the situation.

"True." He narrowed his eyes slightly as if trying to read my mind. "Are you good with that?"

"Yes. Are you?" I countered. Because he wasn't looking pleased about anything.

He sighed then a small tug lifted the right side of his mouth. "Yeah. I just wanted you to myself tonight."

That made me tingly and giddy he wanted me to himself. That meant he had been thinking about me too. Missing me.

"They aren't staying the night," I pointed out, although I understood what he was saying.

"Could the two of you stop eye-fucking each other so we can eat in peace," Micah called out from the end of the table he was now sitting at with a plate of food.

Eli's expression went dark again as he swung his gaze toward Micah, and I grabbed his arm to squeeze it. "Let's eat," I said, trying not to laugh.

"She looks like an angel, but the claws that come out of that one and the mouth will shock you," my brother said to Micah. "You are good at giving it, but if she unleashes, you have met your match." Then Nate pointed his fork at Eli. "That one just hasn't seen it yet. Because if he had, he wouldn't be giving us all that pissed off scowl, but he'd be worried for us."

My brother was pushing it. I shot him a warning glare. I didn't want Eli's family thinking I was a psycho. He laughed and then put a chip with dip in his mouth before winking at me.

Chapter Twenty-Two

~ELI HARDY~

JUNE 15 / 8:57 PM

THE DOOR CLOSED on Crimson as she left my apartment. She'd been the last one to go. The others had started heading out twenty minutes ago starting with Micah and Jude. They had been headed to Live Bay since Larissa was working tonight. Micah had taken her some brownies with him when he left.

Watching Ophelia blend in with my family and how seamlessly her brother being here with Bliss had been, eased my annoyance as the night wore on. The awkwardness I'd been worried about hadn't happened at all. Ophelia had proved she could hold her own with Micah and he had enjoyed the banter too.

When I'd left all of them behind and went to find life outside of this place I'd forgotten things like this. Somehow through it all, I'd grown to think I didn't want this and being done with it all was what I had needed. Tonight, I wasn't so sure anymore.

"That was fun," Ophelia said as she walked over to me from the door, she had opened for my sister because her hands had been full with leftovers and wine.

Fun wasn't exactly the word I would have used to describe it, but I'd enjoyed it okay. Being alone with Ophelia would have been preferable. Having a warning of some sort that they were all going to show up and barge in unannounced would have been better. My youngest sister hadn't been here, and I didn't ask but if Crimson had left her out, then there would be that drama to come from it too.

"This is much better," I replied when she sat down beside me on the sofa.

"I can't argue with that," she said, cuddling up against me. Her hand slid across my stomach and she laid her head on my chest. Any tension I'd been holding onto from tonight was gone that easily. How I'd survived without the effects of Ophelia's presence so long I didn't know. How I'd survive when this ended . . . I couldn't think about.

"Your sister makes really good brownies. I ate two," she said.

"My mom made those. I could tell when I saw them. And you ate three," I replied.

She tilted her head back to look up at me. The amused gleam in her eyes made me want to laugh. "How do you know how many I ate?" she challenged.

I reached over to brush the lock of hair that was about to fall into her eyes out of the way. "I do little else but watch you when you're in a room." There, how was that for honesty.

The way her eyes softened then darkened made my cock harden. She didn't say anything, but after a moment of looking at me with that sultry fuck me gaze, she moved a leg over my lap then lifted herself up with one graceful shift that left her straddling my lap.

I put my hands on her bare thighs. The shorts she was wearing had ridden up and I could slide my hands easily inside the legs until I reached the satin of her panties. But I didn't. I kept my hands just above her knees and waited. She'd made this move and I was going to fucking enjoy every minute of her seduction.

She ran her hands through my hair as her eyes stayed on mine. Her nails slightly scraping my scalp until they reached my neck. Then they left me and with a tug, she pulled her shirt off and dropped it beside us on the sofa. I didn't even get to appreciate the view before she was pulling at my shirt. I lifted my arms and leaned up to help her in undressing me. When it was gone, she started getting rid of her bra. My attention was caught up in that process and I watched in awe and adoration as her breasts bounced free of the lace.

I wasn't going to be able to wait on her next move, not with those perfect pink tipped full tits that close. Reaching up, I cupped them one in each hand and massaged each nipple with the pad of my thumb. She made a sound of pleasure and arched her back to give me complete access.

I slid my hands behind her back and pushed her closer until my mouth was close enough to taste the sweetness in front of me. Ophelia began to rock in a rhythm that pressed her clit directly on the bulge in my jeans. She was panting and softly repeating my name among other things. Everything else forgotten but the building pressure inside of her. She was going after the release and I had a front row seat to the event.

I trailed kisses along her collarbone and the side of her breast. It was for my own pleasure though. Ophelia was almost to her climax and her eyes were closed as she began to ride my lap harder. I lifted my head to watch as the first tremor coursed through her body. Her hands grabbed onto my shoulders, her mouth falling open as she cried out, and her bouncing tits began their own erotic jiggle with her trembling body.

I memorized her like this. Every detail of her face, the curve of her neck, the valley between her breasts. I wasn't romantic. Not anymore. I was a realist. But in that moment, I was positive Ophelia Finlay was the most beautiful creation on Earth.

Watching as she came back to me and her eyes blinked several times while a slow smile spread across her lips, I knew I'd never be the one to walk away from her, but one day she'd leave me. Her beauty wasn't enough to heal the damage inside me.

"I may have been dealing with some pent up sexual tension," she said as her flushed cheeks darkened. She ducked her head then and laughed softly at herself before leaning forward and resting it on my shoulder.

Enjoying having her this close and holding her against me, I pressed a kiss to the top of her head and inhaled her coconut scent. "I'm not complaining. It was one of the most erotic things I've ever experienced."

Ophelia leaned back and looked up at me skeptically. "My humping you like a teenager was erotic?" she asked with a touch of humor.

I shrugged. "The complete unrestrained pleasure I watched you get lost in was by far the most erotic thing I've seen."

The corners of her full lips lifted, and she studied me. I saw when her eyes began to go from amused to sultry. When she began to move from her perch on my lap, I wanted to grab her and hold her there but the way she was looking at me I decided to let her do whatever it was she was thinking about.

She stood up in front of me and started to slide her shorts down her hips then with a little sexy shake they fell to the floor. With a nudge from her foot, she moved them aside. Then she knelt down between my legs and looked up at me with a challenge in her gaze.

I was afraid to breathe.

Her hands touched my thighs then she eased them inside until her palms were pressing my inner thighs. With a push, she opened my legs wider then slid her hands up to the snap on my jeans. I was mesmerized as I watched her unzip slowly. That was all she could do without my help. Her gaze lifted back to meet mine and I lifted my hips just enough so she could tug the jeans down along with my boxers.

She stopped when my now completely rigid cock broke free from its confinement. I wasn't sure if she was planning on climbing back on my lap or if she had other ideas when her hands curled around the hot sensitive flesh and began to carefully pump it.

I no longer had to remind myself to breathe. The quick deep intake of oxygen was the first of many. I didn't want to close my eyes and miss the sight of her hand on my dick. Her long blonde hair resting against my thighs and her breasts brushing the insides of my thighs. My thoughts kept going to her climbing on me again and getting to slide up into her tight wet pussy while she bounced and rocked on me. I throbbed thinking of how amazing it would be to unload inside her like that.

Just when I was about to tell her to get back on me, her head lowered and before I had time to register what she was doing, the warmth of her breath touched the tip of my cock, her plump lips slid down over it, her slick wet tongue playing along the veins bulging until I felt the head hit her throat. The slight choking sound she made caused all rational thought to fade.

"FUCK!" I groaned and grabbed her head to hold it there. That didn't stop her though. Her head began to bob up and down as she wrapped a hand around the base of my dick. The sounds of her sucking were driving me almost as crazy as the feel of it all.

My head fell back on the sofa and I fought to catch my breath, but Ophelia then sucked hard on my oversensitive head. "GOD!

Yes, baby. Suck it," I encouraged. No other thought able to penetrate. I was gone. Completely in her control. She owned me with her mouth.

The end of her tongue ran up the side of my erection then she grabbed it again and pumped it before lowering her mouth over it and taking me all the way in again. This time I felt the back of her throat and then some more. She was gagging as she pushed it deeper. Motherfucker she was going to kill me in the best possible way.

"Holy fuck, baby, that's it. Take it all," I growled as I spoke and grabbed her hair to push her farther down. She moaned then and the way the vibration on my dick felt caused me to begin to shake. This was too fucking incredible. I wasn't ready for it to end, but it was almost there. I didn't know how much more of the sweet torture I could take before I exploded.

She began kissing the head then running her tongue around it. I tried to catch my breath, but there wasn't enough time because she was sucking me in harder this time. Aggressively. As if this excited her. JESUS! That was going to send me over the edge.

"I'm about to come, baby," I warned her.

She became wilder while squeezing the base with her hand as if she was hungry for it. The sight of her taking me into her mouth so desperately was it. I couldn't take any more.

"FUCK!!" I roared and just as my release burst free, she moved her head back and used her hand to shoot my load all over her bare chest. My body jerked almost violently as I watched my semen cover her. "GAAAAH!" was my last shout before I fell back onto the sofa gasping for air.

Chapter Twenty-Three

♥ OPHELIA FINLAY ♥

JUNE 16 / 11:28 AM

THERE WAS A slight part of me that felt guilty for monopolizing Eli's weekend, but it was very small. I was more selfish than I'd realized. I knew he had to get a job and tomorrow he'd be taking his gran to chemo then staying with her the rest of the day. Still when I mentioned leaving so he could get things done he hadn't wanted me to go and I didn't argue.

After breakfast then sex in the shower, we'd decided to come out and lay on the beach. I needed some sunshine. Being lazy on the sand with Eli sounded perfect. However, we hadn't been out here long when my brother had called him and said he had a job he might be interested in. Eli had asked me if I was okay with him leaving to go see what Nate had in mind while Bliss kept me company. Of course, I'd rather be with Eli but if he got a job, then I would stop feeling guilty from keeping him from looking.

I wanted to ask him about where he had been working before,

if he was going back to it, and about where he had been living. But I didn't because I was scared of the answer. If he said they were holding his job for him or that he'd have a place to live when he returned, that would mean I'd lose him. I knew I should ask. I should be aware of what I was walking into but I'd already leaped right on in and I was in love with Eli.

It was too soon. I'd have made fun of anyone else that told me they were in love with someone they'd just started seeing this recently. I let myself care without any details on his plans. He didn't share them and the fool I was I didn't ask.

"Are you awake?" he asked me, and I turned my head to the side facing him before I opened my eyes.

"Yes," I replied.

"Here come Nate and Bliss," he said, nodding his head in the direction behind me. "I need to go inside and get changed."

I was already missing him and he was right here. I knew it wasn't the short amount of time he was going to be gone today that had me feeling this way but the future. When he'd go. Questions I wouldn't ask because I was too scared of the answers.

"Okay," I said smiling even though my chest felt heavy from the direction of my thoughts.

He studied me a moment then glanced back at them before asking me, "What's wrong?"

I was great at avoiding things but terrible at guarding my facial expressions. "Nothing," I lied.

He didn't look convinced. I couldn't say I blamed him since that hadn't sounded entirely convincing.

"Guy I'm taking you to meet would probably rather you wore a shirt." Nate's voice interrupted anything else that could have been said. I was relieved he was here now.

"Jeans might be nice too," Bliss added with a teasing lilt to her voice.

Eli barely glanced at either of them as he continued to study me before he finally stood up. "I was headed in to get dressed," he said, his tone sounded tense. I hated that I was the reason he wasn't more welcoming.

"Do you mind if I join you?" Bliss asked. She was wearing a poppy blue swimsuit with a white see-through cover-up. A beach bag that matched her swimsuit was on her shoulder.

"I'm happy to have the company," I assured her. I must have been mimicking Eli's frown unknowingly.

She turned toward my brother and went up on her tip toes to kiss him. I glanced away while he slid his hand around her waist. I didn't want to stare at their little affectionate embrace.

Eli didn't come over and kiss me, touch me, or anything for that matter. He simply walked back toward the apartment not even waiting on Nate to follow. I kept my eyes on the waves wishing I didn't feel so disappointed, or hurt was probably a better way to describe it.

Eli and I were not what Nate and Bliss were. Comparing the two was unfair. But was my wanting what they had wrong? Couldn't I want that too? Wanting it with Eli was the biggest issue. He was all I wanted but I knew very little about the past year of his life.

How dangerously I'd fallen for him without any walls to protect me.

Bliss took the seat beside me that Eli had vacated. There was a large umbrella between the two chairs but leaning more in my direction than hers. Eli had only mentioned that Nate knew a man who owned restaurants and needed a bartender at the one that was just opened in Pensacola. Eli had a degree in business, but he wasn't looking for a permanent job. Something he could go and do then leave when the time came.

The man Nate was referring to was my uncle Cope's business

partner. I didn't say that to Eli since he hadn't said anything about who it was and I thought there could be a reason Nate left that out. I figured he'd find out when he got there about the family connection.

I glanced over at Bliss and at that moment some other force took over my mouth. Because I surprised myself by blurting out, "Do you know where all Eli went and what he did this past year?"

Bliss seemed a little shocked by my sudden outburst too, but she recovered quickly as a frown formed not only on her mouth but in her eyes. There was worry there and concern. That didn't make me feel better about anything. This was what happens when you ask questions. You find out things you don't want to know.

"No, he's definitely . . . different," she paused, and I could see the uncertainty in her eyes. Either she knew something, or she was reluctant to talk about Eli like this. As if their friend code said they couldn't. I let her think it over and finally she sighed. "I don't know this Eli. There is . . . there was . . . whatever happened with him this past year was bad."

That got my attention. I sat up straighter. She wasn't going to say something like that and let it go. "Why do you think it was bad?" I probed.

She looked down at her hands that were clasped together in her lap. "Eli has always been a rule follower, but he has saw the good in everyone. He was positive. He believed in things. He had"—she glanced up at me and said—"hope."

I waited as she seemed to think about it some more. Although I hadn't known Eli that well before, I could see what she was saying. The guy I'd been around a few times had appeared to be all those things.

"There is a sorrow at times then an emptiness at others when I look at him now. He rarely smiles. He has secrets, Ophelia. I can see them there behind his dark gaze and I love him like my own brothers. I always will no matter how he changes. But I don't want you hurt."

The words "probably a little too late for that" popped in my head.

"You don't think the darkness is about his grandmother?" I asked, knowing it wasn't all of it even if it was some.

Bliss inhaled deeply then gave me such a sad look my chest ached. "No, I don't. Eli was the brightest most positive person in my life when I was battling cancer. He never allowed any negativity. He talked about the future like it was a given. That's the Eli I know. This pain inside him was there before he came back. It had changed him already."

I would have to ask him. If I was going to love this man, I needed to know what had changed him. Even if asking him caused me to lose him. The deeper I sank, the harder this would be. How did I love this man so much yet I didn't completely know him?

Chapter Twenty-Four

~ELI HARDY~

JUNE 20 / 8 AM

I WAS AWAKE contemplating a run for the first time since Alice's death when the phone rang. It was early and my mood lightened as I walked over to pick it up from beside the bed where I'd left it charging. The thought of hearing Ophelia's voice made me hopeful. I'd woken up with my thoughts on her. My dreams had been sweet instead of the nightmare that had once plagued me every time I closed my eyes. She was solely to thank for that even if she didn't know it.

The Atlanta phone number that lit up my screen made all the peace vanish as quickly as it had come. In its place came the heaviness that I tried so hard to push back into a dark corner and forget. The number I had deleted from my contacts months ago, but it was burned into my memory. I recognized it. I'd seen it so many times over the past six months.

That part of my life was over. I had closed the connection.

Ended all attempts at trying to understand. There was nothing that could make the truth easier. None of it had been real. It had been a façade and, in the end, taken the only real thing it had given me. My son.

I ended the call without answering, dropped the phone on the bed this time just as quickly as I had picked it up wanting to get away from the memory. The need to run was now clawing at me in a way it never had. Walking back to the closet, I grabbed the running shorts that had been neglected for so long. Once I had run daily for fitness but the need to run from the demons that I would never be free from pushed me now. The phone call reminding me of what I'd never forget. Choices I could never go back and change.

I'd come to rely on Ophelia to keep me from getting lost in the horror that haunted me. Ophelia couldn't always be here when the memories came. She made me feel centered and I was depending on her presence more and more every day. It was unfair to her. I had to find my own salvation from the past. Being with her shouldn't be based on her easing the pain. I was using her, and I had to find a way to stop. Relying on someone else to cope with anything was unhealthy. The more I told myself this, the deeper my need for her grew.

The phone rang again. I didn't move, standing still, unable to look in the direction of the phone I listened to each ring waiting for it to end. When the last ring faded, I exhaled. I didn't go check the number. I didn't want to see it. Grabbing my running shoes, I put them on and laced them tightly. Before I was finished with this task, the chime alerting me to a voicemail broke the silence. The pounding in my head began. It was a familiar reaction. I inhaled deeply and exhaled preparing for the sorrow to pull at me.

When only the bearable ache lingered inside me at the memory, I took another deep breath. It was confusing and almost relieving. My panic had been a habit. Seeing any reminder from my past had always triggered so many emotions I'd expected it to take over like it always had. This time the power of it was weak. The struggle to breathe hadn't plagued me. I was standing here in my room alone and I was normal.

Walking over to the phone, confused by the ability to suddenly handle something that normally triggered the pain, I felt stronger. Able to face the memory. No longer hiding from it all but accepting it. I picked up my phone and pressed the voicemail notification. Putting it to my ear, I heard the familiar voice I expected.

"It's Annie, but you know that. I have some things of Alice's you might want . . . and Eli, there is something you also need to see. I can't make you talk to me. But you need to see this and see the truth. Hating her won't change the past. She paid for it all with her death. Shit. Whatever. Just call me back."

I stood there after the message had ended. Annie was Alice's older sister. Their voices so similar yet that was where their similarities ended. Annie was a dependable, stable, hard-working single mom, who didn't let her childhood affect the person she had become. It had made her determined and not a victim.

Alice had been the beauty of the two, yet she'd chosen a much different path. One that appeared exciting and colorful yet had been a tragedy wrapped in a shiny package. I'd been fooled by it as had so many. The memory of having to identify her body in the hospital morgue no longer caused me the agonizing grief it should. She had been my wife. Losing her should have been something that would always carry sorrow. But it wasn't sorrow I felt toward Alice's memory. It was anger. Her lies, her choices, her selfish and reckless behavior had taken not just her life but that of our child's. My world had been ripped apart the night I was handed the tiny little boy barely developed wrapped in a blanket with eyes that would never open to this world. They'd tried to save him when they knew Alice wasn't going to survive but it had been too soon for him. He wasn't ready. All the work the doctors and nurses had done couldn't make his body ready to face life outside of the womb. He'd been gone before he entered it.

My gran had always said that secrets never were the winners at hide and seek. It had taken me years to figure out what she meant by that. But when Alice's secrets had no longer had a hiding place those words of my gran's suddenly were very clear. In death, you can't cover up the lies left in your wake. They have a way of unraveling and bursting free to damage everyone in their path.

The man driving the car that had crashed fatally that night killing him on impact and Alice a few hours later was her high school boyfriend. The text messages on her phone revealed a life Alice lived I had never known. Sex so twisted it sickened me and drug use I'd been too fucking naïve to recognize. The things she'd exposed our son to, I would never know. She hadn't even given him a chance. The drugs he'd been exposed to while in her womb were very likely the reason he was underdeveloped for twenty-six weeks.

I'd spent hours researching babies who had been born that early and survived. Trying to find a reason why my son hadn't. Any reason other than the fact his mother had failed him. I had so much to hate her for I wanted to be able to forgive her for something if not everything. In the end, that had been a futile task. It had been me I realized that I hated. Because I hadn't seen the warnings. I hadn't saved our son.

I wouldn't call Annie back. We had said all there was to say to one another the weeks after Alice's death. Annie thought her sister had paid the price for her sins with her life, but I disagreed. She didn't suffer the heart-wrenching sorrow of losing our child. She hadn't held the lifeless infant in her arms and saw his ending before he ever had a beginning. She hadn't faced her sins. She'd escaped all the repercussions for them. I'd been left here to find a way to live through each unraveling of her demented lifestyle. It had been me that was continuously punched in the gut with one truth after another. Each one growing more horrible as the last.

I hadn't gone to Alice's funeral. I hadn't allowed our son to be buried with his mother. Annie was the only family Alice had other than me. She had fought me on it but not hard and not long. She knew there was no point. I wouldn't budge and, in the end, I refused her calls. I didn't even know who had gone to my wife's funeral and to this day I didn't care. Her life had not been one to memorialize.

Alice had failed our child and he deserved more than being buried with a woman who had never protected him. He was pure where she was tarnished even deeper than I had realized. The ugliness that she had allowed to control her in this life had taken her in death and I wanted my son to be in a safe place. It was the only thing I had left to do for him. At that time, it made sense. It was the only way I could see them lower him into the ground. Knowing she was nowhere near him.

I hadn't taken any of Alice's things when I left the apartment we had shared. I'd moved into hers when we had married, leaving things in mine due to the year lease on the place. Grate had been going to sublease it for his girlfriend but that never had time to take place. I'd been back before the ink had been dry on our marriage certificate.

Alice had entered my world like a force of nature. I'd never known anyone like her, and I had thought what we had was the love others searched for. She was always laughing and smiling. I had been drawn to that the first night I met her. In the end, she had been a master manipulator and I had been the idiot who believed she was real. The warning in Annie's words the night we ran off to Vegas to get married were possibly the only truths I'd been given from either of them. I hadn't listened. Believed as Alice had told me so many times that her sister was always jealous of her. She didn't want to see her happy because she was miserable. It had been easy to believe because I wanted it to be true. Alice was pregnant with my child and marrying her had been the next step. Even if there was doubt trying to edge its way in, I had forced it out just like I had chosen not to believe Annie's warning.

Remembering was easier I realized as I stood there letting it all replay like a movie reel in my mind. I had worked so hard at forgetting. Not allowing it to resurface, afraid of the darkness that always came to pull me under. There was the ache that would never go when I remembered the son I had lost. I wanted that memory and I held onto that pain. Some sorrow was meant to stay. The hatred I held for Alice was what I didn't want to allow to control me anymore. Holding onto that kind of anger and hate kept you from living.

"I loved a woman that didn't exist," I said aloud, needing to hear the words. Admitting it and accepting it was like a weight lifted from my shoulders. Forgiving her might never come but letting go of the memory of what I thought she was made the emptiness inside me fade away. The love I'd had for Alice was never real because I hadn't known the woman she truly was. My inability to think about her, about the past had kept me from accepting it for what it was. A freedom came with letting Alice go. The last words Annie had said to me was, "Alice had been chasing death since we were kids." I had hated her for so many things but hating a woman who was damaged since childhood was pointless. It had been me who ignored the truth.

I opened the drawer beside my bed. The box I had placed in there had been unopened since I placed the items inside of it six months ago. I'd bought the small slender cedar box at an antique store two days after leaving Sea Breeze. During the first days of my journey while I was trying to figure out what I wanted in life, I had stopped in little towns that intrigued me. Diners, coffee shops, and unique stores that caught my attention filled that first week for me and kept me moving farther away. I had traveled through four states before slowly turning and heading back east until I ended my journey only hours from where it began.

The box had been my first purchase on that trip. I had walked through the store so full of items from my childhood. It had made me homesick and I wondered more than once while examining toys, lunch boxes, and even china that my gran had if I was doing the right thing.

Then I'd seen this box. The words SPREAD YOUR WINGS had been engraved on the top of the box. As if fate had been trying to talk to me and remind me why I was out here on the road, I repeated the words several times then knew I had to buy the box. Back then I'd been a dreamer and believed it had been words meant for me.

Sitting down on the edge of the bed, I opened the box and did nothing else. The photo that sat on top of the papers folded neatly inside still filled me with regret and sorrow. But I knew that was okay. Losing a child wasn't easy and if the pain didn't come with his memory then what kind of man was I? I held onto the way seeing his small face made me feel. It was all I had of him. All I would ever have of him. I didn't touch the photo but simply studied the small face. That night forever marked me. Holding him had made me realize I had never truly experienced real heartbreak. But more than that, he taught me about unconditional love even though he never took his first breath.

Gently, I closed the lid and placed the box back inside the drawer beside the bed where I had always kept it no matter where I lived. However, this time I couldn't close the drawer. I'd been unable to look at the box and face the reality of the contents for so long yet now the thought of putting him away bothered me. I took the box back out and placed it on the nightstand instead. Hiding his memory never made it fade. I never wanted to forget him.

With one long look at the box, I stood and went to run.

Chapter Twenty-Five

♥ OPHELIA FINLAY ♥

JUNE 29 / 6:34 PM

SUMMER CAMP WAS done. Parents had come today to watch their little angels dance and twirl around the room. Kids were registered for the fall classes beginning in August when school resumed. I had smiled more than was necessary and my cheeks were hurting. No amount of coffee had prepared me for the chaos of today.

On my drive there I'd spoken with Phoenix for the first time in over a month. She'd called me and acted as if she hadn't been ignoring my calls. I had been prepared not to correct her or give her advice she didn't want because I knew doing so would make her ignore me for another month. But she was already realizing her mistake. I could hear it in her voice. The guy wasn't what she had hoped he would be. This had been a call to get me to speak to our parents for her without her actually asking me to do it. Phoenix was as stubborn as she was wild. I would talk to Mom on Monday. This weekend, however, was about me and Eli.

Pulling my car into the parking lot of Live Bay made all that exhaustion vanish. It had only been two nights without Eli, but it had felt longer. Being away from him was only getting more difficult. He'd offered to come to me today, but he'd done that last weekend and Wednesday. With his work schedule now in full effect, it wasn't fair to always expect him to be the one to do this drive.

He had worked long shifts Thursday and Friday so he could have off tonight. I'd suggested we eat dinner here and listen to the band they'd been advertising for the past few weeks. It was growing in popularity because the parking lot was already filling up and it wasn't even eight yet which was when they took the stage.

Luckily I was able to get one of the last parking spots in the front. I quickly put on some lip gloss then grabbed my purse before opening the car door. When I stepped out my eyes met Eli's as he was making his way to me. The sight of him excited me. His blonde hair caught up in the breeze showed off the tattoos on his neck. The sleeveless shirt he was wearing also showcased more of his decorated body. His jeans fit loosely at his hips and I wanted to crawl all over him right here with the world watching.

I only took a few steps before he reached me. I opened my mouth to speak but his was covering mine before a word could be uttered. His hands cupped my face in a way that made me feel cherished and desired. Loving this man was easy but not telling him was getting harder every day. Especially when his actions said he felt the same way even if he had yet to say the words.

I held onto his biceps as he thoroughly kissed me, and I enjoyed it. His silent loving. He did this so often in so many ways I wondered if he even realized it. More than one night I had stayed awake trying to decide if I should say the words first. I didn't know what he had been through or why he'd returned with so much pain inside his beautiful eyes, but I did know I rarely even saw glimpses of that darkness now. There was happiness there.

When he ended the kiss, he pressed one last peck on my lips then held my face a moment longer. "God, I missed you." He said the words with so much passion one would think he hadn't seen me in weeks. This was love. I knew it was. Even if he wasn't ready to say it.

"I've missed you too," I replied, the pleased grin on my face didn't bother my tired cheeks at all. My earlier exhaustion was gone, and I was full of the energy being with Eli seemed to bring me.

"You sure you want to eat here?" he asked. His reluctance to be around his friends and family had bothered me at first. I thought it had been me he was trying to hide. But after a few times of them forcing themselves on us, I realized it wasn't that. Eli got annoyed with them. He liked our time together to be just that. Us.

Fitting into his world was important to me though. I wanted those closest to him to like me. Keeping him away from them wasn't going to earn me any points. So I nodded my head. "Yes. Please," I replied. "We don't have to stay all night. Just long enough to eat and hear some of the band. I'd like to dance with you too." I added the last part because I had thought about that earlier today and I wanted to experience it.

He sighed and reached for my hand. "Fine. Let's go eat."

I giggled at his lack of enthusiasm. "I'm starving," I told him.

"They've got the best greasy fried club food in town." His voice still unimpressed.

I wasn't going to let him sulk. This was good for us to get out and be around others. "What's your favorite fried thing on the menu?" I asked.

"Loaded potato skins with crabmeat," he replied immediately.

That sounded delicious. "That'll be a great appetizer."

He chuckled then and looked down at me. "I fucking love how you eat."

I had made him laugh. It was one of my greatest accomplishments and every time he did it, I was filled with warmth. I loved hearing it and knowing I had done that.

"What do you love about the way I eat, Eli Hardy?" I asked in a prim voice.

He shook his head and we continued to the entrance. "Your passion for food."

I was passionate about food. Smiling, I swung our joined hands back and forth. "That's good to know. Because later you can buy me an ice cream cone."

He opened the door and let my hand go so I could walk inside. "Don't I always buy you an ice cream cone?" he asked.

"Yes, but instead of me hinting I want one I can just come right out and say it. Since you love my food passion."

He started to say more when he was interrupted by a, "ELI, GET MY BEER FROM LARISSA!" yelled from across the room. Eli shot an annoyed glance in the direction of the voice. Jimmy Taylor was at a high top with Marcus, Jude, and a guy I didn't know.

Eli didn't walk over to the bar or to the table with his friends. Instead, his hand rested on my lower back and he steered me toward a regular table closer to the entrance.

"Is he drunk?" I asked, studying the table we were obviously avoiding.

Eli shook his head. "No. Just obnoxious."

I was still curious. "Why did he tell you to get his beer?"

"With Jimmy, it could be a number of reasons."

That wasn't a real answer. I was going to ask another question when Micah's much closer voice stopped me. "He pissed off Larissa. She's withholding his drinks."

I turned in my seat to see Micah approaching us. He gave me a nod hello then gave his attention back to Eli. "Got a minute?" he asked. Micah rarely looked so serious. Come to think of it, I had never seen him appear so . . . concerned?

I kept my focus on Micah trying to figure out what was wrong, but I felt Eli's gaze on me and glanced over at him instead.

Eli appeared annoyed as he gave me an "I told you this was a bad idea" look then glanced back at Micah. "Sure. What?" he drawled sounding as annoyed as he appeared.

There was a pregnant pause and it was awkward. I shifted in my seat nervously.

"Best if we step outside. It's a, uh, private matter." He said the words with such intent I was now getting worried.

That got Eli's attention too. He frowned and said nothing as he stared up at Micah. I knew he was trying to decide if this was important or not.

"I'm fine," I assured him in case he wasn't moving or saying anything because he would have to leave me if he stepped outside.

It was clear he didn't want to go but the way Micah was looking at him, we both knew he needed to go.

"I won't be long," he told me before standing and following an already retreating Micah to the door. I waited until they had disappeared and the large wooden door had closed behind them to let out the breath I was holding. What could that be about?

A dread settled in my gut and I tried to ignore it but the feeling only grew.

Chapter Twenty-Six

~ELI HARDY~

JUNE 29 / 7:02 PM

GRAN. THIS WAS about Gran. My stomach knotted as I followed Micah out into the parking lot. He continued walking until we were around the back of the building. Very few cars were back here this early in the evening. It was private. That was for sure. I fought the urge to tell him to say it already. To stop fucking walking. We were alone for the love of God. What could possibly be this damn personal?

The back door to the club opened and I was expecting Larissa to walk out to join us. For a brief second, I thought he'd walked me back here to talk to her. Let her tell me whatever it was.

But it wasn't Larissa.

Annie stood there looking years older than the last time I had seen her six months ago. It took a moment to let her presence here where she didn't belong sink in. I was thrown off balance as a part of that world walked into my world here. Anger didn't simmer slowly, it exploded within me. She didn't belong here.

I didn't wait for her to speak. I didn't turn to Micah to find out what the fuck he had to do with this. I turned and began to leave.

"ELI, wait!" Annie's voice called and I cringed at the sound of it. I never wanted to see her or anyone connected to Alice again. They were as dead to me as she was. I didn't stop. I kept walking. "Please, Eli! Please just at least let me give you this. I need to explain, you need—"

I stopped and spun back around to face her. Not wanting to hear another word come out of her mouth. "NO! Do you understand? I said NO! Now get the fuck out of my life. You don't belong here."

"You ignored all my calls. I had to come here," she started again, her face frantic as she glanced at Micah for what? Support? How the fuck did he equate into this anyway?

"Leave," I demanded. "I want nothing of hers. Why the fuck would I? Why would you think I needed to hear anything about her? She is dead. Go home, Annie." I didn't give her time to say more before I began walking away again. I didn't head toward the path that would take me back to the front of the building. I couldn't go in there now. I needed to be alone. I needed to get the fuck away from it all.

Just a moment to calm down.

"The baby wasn't yours." Annie had said the words loud enough for me to hear her without yelling. I heard them, but that didn't make what she had said clear. I stopped and stood there for a moment. I didn't turn around again to look at her. There was no point. It was her words I was trying to make sense of.

"JT had wanted her to get an abortion. I found the paperwork for her consultation at the clinic. The night you met her, they were on one of their many breakups because she wasn't getting the abortion. I found a letter she'd written to him but never sent.

It was written the day y'all ran off to get married. She told him she'd found her baby a father. She was going to stay clean and she wanted him out of her life."

I didn't want to hear any more of this. It wasn't true. I had lost my son already. She wasn't going to take his existence from me too. I shook my head and kept walking. This was more of the O'Conner lies. That's all they knew to do. Lie. Destroy everything around them.

"Do the math, Eli. Add it up. The doctors thought the baby could live. She was almost six months pregnant. Not four. Did you even ask about that? The night you met Alice she was pregnant."

Unable to listen to any more of her lies, I turned and stalked back toward her. My fury building as the words continued to spew out of her. "NO! You won't take him from me! I have only that and you want to take it too. He was all that was pure all that was real within the fucking web of lies she destroyed me with." The torment that had held me captive for so many dark days after I'd buried my son was there again. Wrapping me tightly. Reminding me of all that I had lost and how I'd let him down.

Annie didn't move and I stood there now feet away from her wanting to see her walk away. Just fucking disappear.

"I didn't come to cause you more pain," she said slowly. "I came here to free you. To tell you what I should have already done. To save you from the lies that she left behind."

I took a step back from her. The pity in her eyes wasn't meant for me. I wouldn't accept that. Just like her words were bullshit.

"She was my wife. That was my son. The rest was a lie. Our life had been one big motherfucking lie. But I held him. MY son, damn you. He was mine. You won't take that from me too." Every word from me burned like acid in my throat. I saw the truth in her eyes and my chest felt like a fire had exploded inside me.

Without another word, I went to my bike. I didn't look back

and I rode away. From the lies, from the truth, from everything that I'd been running from since the night Alice died, from Sea Breeze . . . and from the only hope I had at living again.

Chapter Twenty-Seven

♥ OPHELIA FINLAY ♥

JUNE 30 / 12:07 AM

ITTING IN FRONT of the dance studio when I pulled up after my drive back from Sea Breeze was the last person I expected to see. I'd hoped in the dark corners of my broken heart that Eli might be here waiting. The small shred of hope that when he had driven off, he'd needed to leave everyone else, but he would find his way back here. He wasn't here though, and the tears still wet on my cheeks did nothing to ease the pain he'd inflicted. Not from the words I'd heard outside Live Bay but from his leaving without saying anything. I thought we were something more. That he'd explain it all to me, tell me the whole story. But I'd been wrong, and the heartbreak was like anything I had ever experienced.

I turned off my car, but I didn't get out. I sat in the silence and studied my sister sitting on the cement with her legs crossed and her back resting against the front door to the dance studio.

There was a suitcase beside her, and I knew then her relationship had ended. This was her return. Her eyes met mine and even in the limited lighting, I could see the dark circles under them. Her fair skin was more pale than normal. Phoenix was dealing with hurt as well. It was clear in her eyes.

I wanted to curl up and cry until I was too tired to cry anymore, but my sorrow would have to wait. I could see without hearing her say a thing that my sister needed me. She was carrying her own pain inside and like always she was coming to me to unload it. I'd have to listen, advise, and give her a shoulder to cry on. My tears had to be put on hold. Taking a deep breath, I wiped away what was left of them on my cheeks and did the best I could to compose myself and get a firm lock on my emotions before getting out of the car.

Phoenix stood up as I walked toward her. She had lost some weight which was unnecessary and made her appear fragile. My sister was not a fragile person. She was headstrong, determined, outspoken, extroverted, and at times mean as hell. She was by no means fragile. However, right now she appeared to be and that worried me. I had never seen her like this.

"What's wrong with you?" I asked her as I stopped in front of her and then grabbed her chin so I could study her thin, pale, face closely. When she didn't jerk away from me with a smartass comment, I knew this must be bad. She was not okay. This was not my feisty sister.

"I've been sitting on that hard concrete for two hours and my butt is sore. What's wrong with you?" was her reply. That sounded more like Phoenix even if she didn't currently look like the smartass she was, at least there was fight left in her.

"I fell in love with a man who doesn't love me, he had secrets, I knew he did, the secrets came out tonight, he ran off without a word, I don't know when I will see him again. Now what happened to you?" I knew my sister well enough to know she'd evade answering until she had the Cliff Notes on why my eyes were red and swollen. I wasn't a crier.

She frowned. "You fell in love with Eli Hardy?" she asked, sounding shocked.

"Yes, but I didn't tell you his name," I pointed out.

"Nate told me you were seeing him," she explained. Then she sighed so heavily her thin shoulders lifted dramatically before falling back into the slump they were in before. "He was married," she said.

Yes, I had heard Eli was married. The woman outside Live Bay had said as much. How on earth did Phoenix know that? "How did you know about Eli's marriage?" I asked confused and suddenly feeling even more lost.

Her eyes widened and her jaw dropped. "Holy shit," she said then continued to gape at me. My confusion was mounting. "Eli Hardy is married?"

"Wait . . . you didn't know Eli was married then who were you talking about?" I asked, realizing then she hadn't been talking about Eli when she had stated he was married. Even as I worked through it all in my head, it began to become clear. "Oh no," I said, understanding now what Phoenix had been telling me.

"Yeah, he told me yesterday morning. When I walked into the apartment to find his wife there. She was surprising him. Her and their two little boys." Phoenix's voice sounded void of emotion, but her eyes told a different story.

"Bastard," I said angrily, thinking of how he'd not only used my sister but he'd cheated on his family. There was no reason to continue this outside. I wrapped my arm around her shoulders and pulled her against me in a hug before unlocking the door and opening it for her to go inside. "Is that suitcase all you have?" I asked her as she picked up the handle to roll it.

"It's all I took the time to get."

I didn't press her for more. Once she was inside and headed for the loft entrance, I locked the door behind me and followed her in silence. My broken heart still throbbed painfully in my chest. Tears still clogged my throat as I thought of Eli and the desire to see him. Hold him. The fear I may never get a chance to do that again gripping me so tightly in my chest it hurt to breathe.

I couldn't dwell on that now though. Phoenix was not the one to unload on. She wasn't very good at support. I held my sorrow inside. For now, I would focus on hers and allow it to distract me.

When we were inside the apartment, Phoenix left her suitcase by the door and walked over to the sofa and sank down onto it. I laid the keys on the entry table and waited for her to say something. I could tell she wanted to unload.

"I'm pregnant," she said the words as she stared straight ahead at nothing.

"Oh no." I could only manage a whisper. She'd said the only thing I hadn't been expecting to hear. Unable to move, I stood there staring at her wondering if I'd heard her incorrectly.

"I told him at the airport. I'd been going to tell him tonight. I was planning a surprise dinner and," she paused, closed her eyes and shook her head. "I was so stupid. I thought he would be excited. I thought we were in love." Finally, she turned to look at me. "But we weren't. he has a family already. A beautiful family."

I moved to her then. She was so close to breaking down and I had no words of comfort, but I wanted to hold her. I didn't want her to feel alone. Sitting down beside her, I reached for her hand and held it in both of mine. The first tear slid free and rolled down her cheek.

"She didn't even acknowledge me. She looked at me once then back at him and said 'This again? Really Edward? I thought we had moved past your need for a toy. Make it disappear please.'

Then she had taken her boys' hands and told them to go find a bedroom they liked. As if I weren't standing there. As if I was a pet he'd picked up. In that moment, all I could think was 'His name is Edward?'" She laughed, but it wasn't real. It was more hysterical. "I thought it was Dannon. Like the yogurt."

My father may kill the man. I hoped he was wealthy enough to hide properly.

The first sob broke free and Phoenix turned and laid her head on my shoulder as she cried. I held her and said nothing. There was nothing I could say to make this better. I had no wisdom for her. No guidance. My little sister's bad decisions had always been an issue. This time, however, she'd have to grow up. There would be no more time for selfish impulsiveness. Those days had ended.

My tears returned and I cried silently as she clung to me. This time I wasn't just crying for myself, but for the life my sister had to face now. She was terrified and no one could fix that for her. I would sit here and hold her until she had no tears left. Then put her to bed. Tomorrow we would decide how to tell my parents.

Chapter Twenty-Eight

~ELI HARDY~

JULY 5TH / 8:17 AM

I HAD JUST finished drying my hair with a towel when the doorbell rang. I knew someone would come by today. I was expecting one or both of my parents. The family Fourth of July gathering had been yesterday at Gran's and I'd not gone. I had seen Gran early that morning and explained to her that I had to work. She understood and although I knew she had questions, she hadn't asked them.

Dropping the towel on the sink, I went to open the door and deal with this now rather than later. If my dad needed to yell at me, or my mother fuss then ask me a million questions it was time I let them do that. I'd been avoiding everyone for a week. They probably knew something now but not enough about my past.

Larissa walked past me before I even got the door fully opened. "You've had enough time. I respected you had to deal with things. I kept my mouth shut as did Micah. But you're going to look at these damn papers that woman left right fucking now. Then we are going to accept what it says and if you need to get drunk, we will do that. This hiding away shit stops though. You have family and friends who love you. Stop avoiding them. Let us help you heal, goddamnit!"

Larissa opened the leather bag she had on her arm and pulled out papers that had been folded. I watched her silently as she opened them up and looked at them. "I've already seen this, and I know what it says. From the shit I heard out behind Live Bay a week ago, I was able to piece this all together. YOU need to look at this." She shoved the papers at me.

I didn't argue with her. She was right, I needed to see what it was Annie had brought for me. It had taken some time to let it sink in, but I knew she'd been telling the truth. With or without whatever this was she had left for me. The papers were from a women's clinic in Atlanta. The papers confirmed Alice's pregnancy. It stated she was four weeks pregnant. There was a helpline for addiction and a list of several abortion clinics. The papers were important because of the one thing on them that Annie had circled with a red marker—the date.

The visit had been three days after I met Alice.

I had already accepted this. The baby boy I had held in my arms, the name Isaac Hardy I had given him, had never been mine. Even now that I knew he had been a part of another lie Alice had told me, it didn't change how I felt about him. Isaac was a Hardy. I'd been the only parent to hold him. I'd been the only person at his memorial. I was all he ever had. I was the one person on this earth who mourned for him and loved him.

That alone made me his father.

All this paperwork did was tell me Alice had been lying from the very beginning. There had never been real love between us. I loved someone who never existed. I didn't know the real Alice.

I had married a girl because I thought she was pregnant with my child. I believed I loved her. In reality, I had fallen in love. With the baby she carried inside her.

"Are you okay? Do I need to get the whiskey?" Larissa asked me, her voice softer now. Not in command mode like she had been when she walked inside here.

"I'm okay. I'd already accepted this. Annie showing up like she did and blindsiding me with it had been necessary. I get it now, but this was something I think deep down I knew and I was running from the truth because I wanted him to be mine biologically," I explained. "But it took me some time alone to face this and accept. I've done that and out of all the lies Alice spun and the destruction she left behind, she can't take away how I felt holding Isaac in my arms. I grieved for the life he would never have because I loved him. I was the only person who did and that makes him mine. I was also his." I handed the papers back to Larissa. "You can have these. They hold facts, but those facts don't change how I feel about him."

Larissa took the papers then took two steps back to sit down into the chair behind her. "Shit. Now I need a fucking drink," she said, reaching up to wipe a tear that had rolled down her cheek.

"I can make you coffee," I offered.

She looked up at me and gave me a watery, emotional smile. "Is it bad that I hate this bitch? She's dead. You shouldn't hate the dead. Right?"

I understood hating Alice too well. I'd lived seven months hating her, but there was no point in that. Not anymore. "She's dead. I'm not. I have a life to live the best way I can. Why hate her because she lost the chance to change her ways? She lost the chance to choose to be a good person. The short life she had started with horror and instead of finding a better life like her sister did, she died in horror as well. I can't hate her because she was never well mentally."

Larissa leaned back in the chair. "You're a good man, Eli Hardy," she said with a touch of pride in her voice. "No amount of tattoos or moody asshole decisions can change the good in you. Try and cover it up all you want but you will never be a bad boy. Get over it."

None of that had to do with me trying to be someone I wasn't. Circumstances had caused me to change. The truth was I wanted to be a good man. My dad had a great life and he was never a hell-raiser. Being bad for fun never appealed to me.

"I'll never be the same guy who left here again. Too much happened and it changed me but I'm not going to let it ruin me. Not anymore. I'm not weak and it's time I remember that." I said the words I'd been telling myself the past few days aloud. Hearing them helped solidify that decision.

"That's a relief," she said, looking pleased. "What about Ophelia? Have you talked to her? Fixed shit there?"

I shook my head. It was all I could do. Saying her name was difficult. She was always on my mind. Every decision I made, her voice was there in my head. My dreams were always of her. She would be the one who taught me that loving a woman was more than sappy emotions, attraction, shared memories, hot sex, and the way you felt around her. Really loving a woman was wanting her bad moods as much as her good ones, craving the sound of her voice even when you can't stand the thought of speaking to anyone, finding peace in her presence when you thought you'd never find a way free of the sorrow, loving a woman is when holding her is all you need. Loving a woman also meant acknowledging when you hadn't treated her the way she deserved and letting her find the man worthy of her. Ophelia Finlay would forever own my heart. While she had given unselfishly, I'd allowed my inner turmoil to ignore what she deserved.

I walked past Larissa without another word. I'd make coffee, I'd go to see my gran, and I'd go to work. I would live my life and find where I fit here once again. No matter where she was or what she was doing, I knew I'd also love Ophelia Finlay with every fiber of my being until the day I died.

Chapter Twenty-Nine

♥ OPHELIA FINLAY ♥

JULY 8TH / 9:30 PM

I STOOD OUTSIDE of Live Bay in the tightest, shortest dress I owned. My heels were so hot I was obsessed with the way they made my legs look. Bliss had helped me curl my hair and I knew it hung perfectly in loose curls down my back. She'd done such a good job. I owed her big time for putting up with me all afternoon and evening. I'd left the guest bedroom at her house in a mess. Unsure what to wear when I grabbed every dress I owned from my closet, tossed it in my car and drove to Nate and Bliss's house after having a meltdown this morning. I had tried on most of those dresses for Bliss and most of them were tossed all over the bedroom I stayed in when visiting their house.

The past few weeks, I had been consumed with helping Phoenix adjust to her reality. It had helped me during the days not being able to sit home alone and fall apart. However, at night I spent most of those missing Eli and crying. Okay, I spent all of those missing Eli and crying. It wasn't getting better. Time was not easing my heart ache. I was in love with the man and if I had to force him to accept he loved me too, I was going to do it. If I thought about this plan too hard, I would back out of it and I knew that.

Bliss's enthusiasm with my decision had helped keep me on track and not running to a closet to sit alone and weep. She thought this was what Eli needed and she also believed he loved me. I was holding onto that tightly. I wasn't so sure he loved me, but I knew I loved him enough I could wait for him to feel the same way. If he gave us more time, I thought surely he would see how perfect we fit. I just couldn't imagine that the love I had for this man wasn't reciprocated at all. How could I feel so deeply and he feels nothing?

I knew there was bad, painful, things from his last relationship. I'd heard enough that night when I'd walked outside to check on things. My heart broke thinking about the son he had lost. I wanted to hold him and tell him I was so sorry and I loved him. If I could take all that pain away, I would. Thinking of all this reminded me why I was here and about the man I had to convince to come back to me.

Never again would I call a woman desperate when she fought for a man who wasn't fighting for her. All my badass belief that if a man didn't want me, then I would walk away and not look back was horse crap when you were truly in love.

I reached for the door and jerked it open then went inside before my nerves could fade again. A live band was on stage and the lights were dim in the crowd, but that helped me feel less on display. I didn't want to draw attention to myself. I just wanted to find Eli. Bliss had to do a little more than nudge my brother to go make sure Eli was here tonight. I had no idea how Nate managed to get him here, but we'd gotten the text an hour ago letting us know he'd be here and that we both owed him big.

Looking in the direction of where Eli and his bunch normally sat, I found my brother immediately because he was watching me. Swinging my gaze from him, I instantly found Eli. He wasn't watching the stage. He was sitting there listening to Micah talk, but he didn't seem interested. I took a deep breath and headed in their direction. I had rehearsed this a million times in my head and there was a very good chance Eli would turn me down, walk away, leave. My stomach started knotting up thinking about it. If he did leave would I chase after him? Was I that crazy and pathetic?

Just before I reached him, his head turned quickly as if someone had alerted him to my approach and his eyes widened as his gaze found me. His eyes slowly took me in and I had never felt so self-conscious in my life. All my earlier confidence seemed to have left me here on my own.

"Hello, Eli." My voice was shaky from my nerves and I hoped the noise in the place masked some of it. "Dance with me," I then blurted out, forgoing all the well thought out flirty things I had been going to say next.

He didn't say anything for a moment then he stood up and I thought this was it. He was about to bolt. My panic began to set in, but before I could grab him and plead, he took my hand in his and led me away from the table but not toward the dance floor either. We were headed to the exit and I felt tears sting my eyes. He wasn't leaving, he was making me leave. What did I do now? Did I just go? Did I beg him to listen to me? Did I tell him I loved him enough for both of us? Oh God, I hadn't thought this through. Not this ending. I wasn't ready for it.

He reached for the door and opened it then led us outside. I was ready to fall apart and cry hysterically. I felt it bubbling to the surface. He wasn't even willing to let me try and persuade him. He was walking me away from everyone . . . toward the road?

I glanced up at him and took an unsteady breath trying to

figure out what we were doing. But he kept walking, looking straight forward and after checking both ways, we crossed the street and then he led us to the wooden bridge that walked over the sand dunes directly to the gulf.

Before we reached the sand, Eli muttered a curse word then moved so quickly I didn't have time to prepare before he had me pressed against him and his mouth covering mine. I needed oxygen, but I craved this more. It gave me hope and my heart felt lighter than it had since he'd rode away without a word. I held onto him and kissed him back with all the love inside me, all the pain from missing him and all the determination to make him stay with me. To love me.

He broke the kiss and took a step back.

I let out a cry from my need to inhale and my panic he was leaving me. Once I had oxygen in my lungs again and could speak, I forgot all the things I had planned to say. Instead, I just let words fly. "I love you. I love you enough for both of us. I will love you even if you can't love me. We make each other happy. That's got to be love, right? You have to feel something. Maybe not what you think you need to feel, but I can wait. I can be patient. I just . . . I want you, Eli. I want to be with you. Please don't leave. Let me show you I can make us work. I'll make you happy." I stopped then and fought back the tears threatening to burst free and make me even more hysterical.

Eli tilted his head to the side as he studied me. I didn't speak in case he was deciding if this option was possible. Maybe something I had said made him think he could love me one day.

"Do you honestly believe I don't love you?"

I understood his words, but the question didn't make much sense. Not coming from him.

"Have I even fucked that up? This"—he waved his hand slowly up and down as he gestured to my body—"this is to get my attention because you think you need to beg me to want you?" He ran a hand over his face roughly. "Jesus Christ, Ophelia. I don't deserve this and I sure as hell don't deserve you." He sounded angry.

"I love you," I repeated. "I will do anything to be with you. To show you how much."

He groaned then and he reached out and pulled me to him. "Please, baby, I need you to stop. You're killing me with every word that comes out of your mouth. I don't fucking deserve you and I thought I was a good man, but I'm not that good. Because a better man would let you go. He'd know you deserve so much more. I was trying to be a better man." He stopped then pressed a kiss to the top of my head then inhaled deeply. "You own me. Every motherfucking corner of my soul is consumed with you. To tell you I love you isn't enough. It's never been enough. But make no mistake, I do love you."

This was real. Not some dream that kept me up at night taunting me with what I wanted most. I held onto him tightly, pressing my face into his chest. His arms flexed as he kept his hold on me. The waves crashed behind us, the sea breeze wrapped us in its warmth. And we stood there knowing this was it. We had both found it. The road hadn't been easy, and the future wouldn't always be smooth. But we had found each other.

"Can you forgive me for not loving you the way you deserved? I swear I'll spend the rest of our lives making sure you never go a day not knowing how much you mean to me."

I tilted my head back then and stared up into his eyes. They were shiny with unshed tears and I saw the good man inside that would always be Eli Hardy. "There is nothing to forgive, but I won't fight you on wanting to show me just how much you love me."

A grin pulled at the corners of his mouth. I licked my lips thinking of how I could kiss that mouth anytime I wanted. "I missed you," I told him.

He sighed and closed his eyes for a second then gazed down at me. "I can swear to you that I missed you more. Being away from you was hell. The only way I got through the day was telling myself I was doing it for you."

"Eli Hardy, I love you, but you are a fool."

He laughed. Loudly. It was real, it was free of darkness, and it was the most beautiful sound in the world.

Acknowledgments

WRITING A BOOK takes so much more than just the author.

There is the editor who has to work around the author's creative issues that can range from anything to last minute changes, missing deadlines, and grammar stupidity. Ellie at *www.mybrotherseditor.net* saved my ass on this one. She worked fast, never complained, and helped me get it ready in time. I love you, Ellie!!!

The formatter is key. Making sure your book is ready to look its best, read easily on ebook or print, and look professional. Christine Borgford is the best. I never want to use anyone else! Thank you so much, Christine, for always working with my short notice requests!!

Special thank you to Danielle Lagasse, Vicci Kaighan, and Jerilyn Martinez. Together they lead Abbi's Army out of the goodness of their hearts. I love them, I love Abbi's Army and all my readers. Without their support, I wouldn't be here.

My family needs a mention because they are the ones who must step in and do the laundry, watch Emerson, find something to eat for dinner and remind me a hundred times that we need toilet paper, milk, laundry detergent, etc.

I love y'all. I have the best kids and parents on the planet.

Britt because even when you weren't here . . . you were. I love you.

ABBI GLINES

Abbi Glines is a #1 New York Times, USA Today, and Wall Street Journal bestselling author of the Rosemary Beach, Sea Breeze, Vincent Boys, Existence, and The Field Party Series . She never cooks unless baking during the Christmas holiday counts. She believes in ghosts and has a habit of asking people if their house is haunted before she goes in it. She drinks afternoon tea because she wants to be British but alas she was born in Alabama. When asked how many books she has written she has to stop and count on her fingers. When she's not locked away writing, she is reading, shopping (major shoe and purse addiction), sneaking off to the movies alone, and listening to the drama in her teenagers lives while making mental notes on the good stuff to use later. Don't judge.

You can connect with Abbi online in several different ways. She uses social media to procrastinate.

www.abbiglines.com
www.facebook.com/abbiglinesauthor
twitter.com/AbbiGlines
www.instagram.com/abbiglines
www.pinterest.com/abbiglines

Other titles by

ABBI GLINES

As She Fades

ROSEMARY BEACH SERIES
Fallen Too Far
Never Too Far
Forever Too Far
Rush Too Far
Twisted Perfection
Simple Perfection
Take A Chance
One More Chance
You We're Mine
Kiro's Emily
When I'm Gone
When You're Back
The Best Goodbye
Up In Flames

SEA BREEZE SERIES
Breathe
Because of Low
While It Lasts
Just For Now
Sometimes It Lasts
Misbehaving
Bad For You
Hold On Tight
Until The End

THE FIELD PARTY SERIES
Until Friday Night
Under the Lights
After the Game
Losing the Field
Making a Play (Coming August 2019)

ONCE SHE DREAMED
Once She Dreamed (Part 1)
Once She Dreamed (Part 2)

THE VINCENT BOYS SERIES
The Vincent Boys
The Vincent Brothers

THE MASON DIXON SERIES
Boys South of the Mason Dixon
Brothers South of the Mason Dixon

THE SWEET SERIES
Sweet Little Thing
Sweet Little Lies
Sweet Little Memories
Sweet Little Bitch

EXISTENCE TRILOGY
Existence (Book 1)
Predestined (Book 2)
Leif (Book 2.5)
Ceaseless (Book 3)

CPSIA information can be obtained
at www.ICGtesting.com
Printed in the USA
LVHW031603260420
654464LV00004B/1378